Shooting by the Sea

A MOLLIE MCGHIE SAILING MYSTERY #5

ELLEN JACOBSON

Shooting by the Sea
Copyright © 2020 by Ellen Jacobson

This book is a work of fiction. Names, characters, places, and incidents either are products of the author's imagination or are used fictitiously. Any resemblance to actual persons, living or dead, events, or locales is entirely coincidental.

Print ISBN: 978-1-951495-11-4
Digital ISBN: 978-1-951495-10-7
Large Print ISBN: 978-1-951495-12-1

Editor: Under Wraps Publishing

First Printing: August 2020

Published by: Ellen Jacobson
www.ellenjacobsonauthor.com

For cats everywhere who can't understand why their humans don't like to roll around in catnip and sleep in cardboard boxes like they do.

CONTENTS

CHAPTER 1
CELEBRITY CRUSH

What would you do if your husband had a crush on a television game show host? Would you:

(a) hide the remote control so that he couldn't watch her show;

(b) sign him up for ballroom dancing lessons to distract him;

(c) talk about your own celebrity crush; or

(d) have a rational conversation about how ridiculous his latest obsession is?

Option (a) might have worked if we lived like normal people in a house.

We're far from normal though. We live on a sailboat at the Palm Tree Marina in Florida. There's barely room on our boat for two people and a cat, let alone a television. So my husband, Scooter, went to the marina lounge when Cassie Newton's show was on. Unfortunately, there are way too many witnesses there for me to hide the remote.

I had mixed feelings about option (b). The Coconut Cove Community Center held ballroom dancing classes, which just happened to be scheduled at the same time as when Cassie Newton's *Triviamania* show aired. The timing was perfect. After our disastrous first dance at our wedding reception, Scooter has always wanted to take lessons, but I've resisted. Klutzes like me don't belong on the dance floor. There are way too many embarrassing photos of me doing a face plant in our wedding cake to prove it.

Instead of ballroom dancing, I could

have tried option (c) and raved about how amazing Jason Momoa looked in *Aquaman*. Except knowing Scooter, it wouldn't have occurred to him to be jealous. My husband has an extensive collection of *Aquaman* comic books and the minute I mentioned Jason Momoa, he would have taken it as an opportunity to talk about what it would be like to live underwater. Mr. Oblivious wouldn't even have considered the fact that I could have had a crush of my own.

Which leads me to option (d)—have a rational conversation with him about his obsession. Though obsessions aren't rational, especially Scooter's. Take, for example, the time he was convinced that we needed not just one ant farm, but twenty-seven of them. It was a total nightmare when they escaped. Or the time he went through a pickled food phase. That one was gross. Have you ever had a pickled marshmallow? I don't recommend it.

Upon reflection, I guess his current obsession with Cassie Newton wasn't so bad. He didn't spend our savings on it, a call to a pest control specialist wasn't required, and he didn't try to serve me pickled Cheerios for breakfast.

Rational conversations with him are best saved for more serious issues, like whether we should get a composting toilet on our boat. Scooter thinks we should. I'm really dubious—the whole idea sounds pretty disgusting. They're basically litter boxes for humans.

See, I told you; we don't live like normal people in a normal house on land with a television and a flushing toilet. Nope, life on a boat can be pretty weird at times. Also, the people who live on boats can be pretty weird too. Especially the ones who are obsessed with Cassie Newton.

So you can only imagine how crazy it

got when Cassie Newton herself made an appearance in our small town of Coconut Cove. Are you curious as to how bizarre it got? Why don't you grab yourself a beverage and some sort of chocolaty treat? Then I'll tell you exactly what happened.

* * *

"We're going to be late." Scooter looked at me sideways as he turned into the parking lot at the Tipsy Pirate.

I frowned. "Well, it's not my fault that Mrs. Moto got into the cupboard and knocked the container of cat food onto the floor. I had to clean it up or else she would have eaten it all while we were gone and then gotten sick."

"We might need to get childproof locks."

"Mrs. Moto is too clever for those," I said. "She'd figure them out in a minute. What we need are cat proof locks."

"Something you need opposable thumbs to operate," Scooter suggested, as he pulled into an empty parking spot.

"I'm not even sure that would stop her. Honestly, she's so smart that she should be on the trivia team instead of me."

"Yeah, she'd ace the 'how to outsmart your humans' category, for sure." Scooter laughed as he turned off the engine. Then he leaned over and kissed me on the cheek. "But I'd much rather have you by my side."

"That's only because I nailed the *Star Wars* question last week."

"Well, that did get us into the semi-finals." His eyes sparkled. "I have a good feeling about our chances. I think we'll be heading to the finals after tonight."

As we walked into the bar, I looked around the room incredulously. The place was jam-packed, even for a Friday night. Were there this many folks interested in watching people answer trivia questions? I shook my head. Probably not. They must be running some sort of special. I rubbed my hands together. Maybe drinks were two for one and they were handing out free appetizers.

Scooter tugged my arm, interrupting my thoughts about whether I should order egg rolls with pineapple dipping sauce or fried cheese balls.

"They're over there," he said, pointing at the center of the room where six tables were cordoned off in front of a small stage.

As we walked over to our table, I nudged Scooter. "Did you see that? People are holding up signs with our team name on them."

He grinned. "There are a lot of folks who want to see the Savvy Sailing Squad emerge victorious."

"And I thought everyone was just here for the free egg rolls."

Ben Moretti and Penny Chadwick—two of our teammates—were sitting at the table closest to the stage. I scanned the room, but didn't see our other team member, Alejandra Lopez.

Penny let out a huge sigh of relief when we sat down. "Boy, am I glad to see y'all. I was starting to worry that you wouldn't make it," she admitted with that adorable Texan twang of hers.

"Sorry, we're late," Scooter said. "Mrs. Moto had a bit of a feeding frenzy."

"She's been eating a lot lately," Ben said. "Maybe she's pregnant."

"She's not pregnant," I said. "She's just greedy. Besides, she's been spayed. There won't be any miniature Mrs. Motos running around. One is more than enough."

"That's too bad," Ben said. "I bet she would have had cute kittens. Calico bobtails, just like her."

"Maybe we should go to the animal shelter and get you a cat of your own," I

said.

"No way." The young man held his hands up. "That's way too much responsibility for me."

"Where's Alejandra?" Scooter asked as he adjusted his tortoiseshell glasses.

"She texted to say that she's running late," Penny said. "Last-minute problems getting the nail salon ready for the grand opening next week."

Scooter blanched. "What are we going to do if she doesn't make it? She's our pop culture expert." He pulled his phone out of his pocket. "I should call her."

I put my hand on Scooter's arm. "Alejandra's probably really stressed out right now. She's been working hard to get everything ready. If she can make it, she will."

"You're right," Scooter said slowly. "It's just that I want the Savvy Sailing Squad to make it through to the finals."

"I know you do. I want us to win too."

Ben snorted. "You don't care if we

win, Mollie. You just want to make sure they lose." He pointed at our rivals, the Barnacle Babes Brigade.

I suppressed a smile. "Well, that might have something to do with it."

"Can I have everyone's attention, please?" a voice boomed out over the speakers.

A woman, probably in her early thirties, was standing on stage holding a microphone and waiting for the audience to quiet down. She wore her dark hair in a tousled bob. It was the kind of look which gives the illusion that you've just ran your fingers through it when you've woken up. Although, in reality, probably took hours to style. Her outfit had the same messy chic look about it, including a cream scarf with a beaded fringe that looked like it had been purposefully wrinkled.

"Hello, my name is Brittany Abernethy," she said. "I'm the executive producer of a little show called

Triviamania. Maybe some of you have heard of it."

While the crowd cheered and clapped, Scooter's eyes grew wide. "Can you believe it? The executive producer of *Triviamania* is here, in Coconut Cove."

"This is awesome," Ben said, clapping Scooter on the back.

Brittany grinned. "From that reaction, I'm guessing some of you watch the show." After another round of applause, she added, "How many of you are Cassie Newton fans?"

Ben let out a whoot-whoot sound. Scooter whistled appreciatively. Penny and I both shrugged.

"Well, then have I got a treat in store for you. Cassie Newton herself is here tonight to emcee the semi-finals."

The crowd went wild. I put my fingers in my ears when Scooter shrieked like a teenage girl in the presence of a favorite pop idol.

When the noise finally died down,

Penny furrowed her brow. "Why is everyone making such a big deal over Cassie Newton?"

I shook my head. "No idea. It's just a TV show."

"*Triviamania* isn't just a TV show," Scooter spluttered. "It's the best thing since—"

Fortunately, Brittany interrupted before Scooter could explain to Penny in detail how wonderful Cassie and her show were. A subject I had been getting tired of hearing about.

"Please join me in giving Cassie a warm welcome to the stage."

The *Triviamania* theme music blared over the loudspeakers while the crowd got to their feet. When the music ended, Brittany smiled and pointed at the stairs to the stage, expecting Cassie to run up them. When the TV host didn't appear, the executive producer's smile faded. Then she turned to the audience, a bright smile plastered back on her face.

"Maybe she's shy," she said. "Should we try this again?"

The music started again, the crowd continued to cheer, and I wondered if it was too late to feign a headache and sneak back home.

When the music ended this time and Cassie still hadn't appeared, Brittany frowned. She motioned a man over and whispered something in his ear. Then she turned back to the audience. "Sorry, folks. She'll be right with us."

The man bustled off to the kitchen. After poking his head inside, he turned back and gave Brittany a thumbs up sign.

She breathed a sigh of relief, and the music started playing again. The man walked back toward the stage, Cassie Newton trailing behind him. She seemed oblivious to where she was, her cell phone pressed against her ear. She must not have liked what the person on the other end said, because her expression darkened as she walked up the steps.

As the last notes of the *Triviamania* theme song played, Brittany tried to get Cassie's attention, but she waved her away. As the music ended, the crowd waited with bated breath to hear from their TV idol.

Cassie held the phone away from her and glared at it. Then she pressed it against her ear again and shrieked loudly enough for people at the rear of the bar to hear clearly, "Don't you dare even think about it. The only way that's going to happen is over your dead body!"

* * *

Cassie looked up, suddenly aware of where she was. While her face reddened, Brittany blinked rapidly.

After a beat, the executive producer smiled. "I bet you didn't know that in addition to being a game show host, Cassie is also a talented actress. Did you enjoy that scene she just played for you? Wasn't that amazing?" She clapped her hands, motioning for the audience to join in. The crowd murmured amongst themselves for a moment, then slowly started applauding.

"Why don't we take a quick break," Brittany said. "Then we'll be back shortly to kick off the semi-finals." She grabbed Cassie by the elbow and briskly steered her off stage.

As they walked past us, I eyed up the TV host. She was an older woman, probably in her sixties, but she had a well-preserved quality about her that was likely due to expensive beauty treatments and perhaps some surgical intervention. She was wearing a simple chambray shirtdress that she had accessorized with a bright yellow snakeskin belt, large hoop earrings, and purple canvas sneakers.

"Did you see her stumble?" Penny whispered to me. "Maybe she's had too much to drink."

"I don't know," I said. "She could have just tripped on something. Happens to me all the time."

While we waited for Brittany and Cassie to return to the stage, Scooter flagged a waitress over and ordered a pitcher of the Tipsy Pirate's famous rum punch for our table. I chimed in and suggested we also get a couple orders of egg rolls and fried cheese balls.

"So, what do you think that was all about?" Penny asked after the waitress bustled off to get our drinks and food.

Scooter cocked his head to one side. "What do you mean?"

"That outburst," Penny said.

"You mean the scene she performed?" Scooter asked.

"It certainly was a scene," I said dryly.

"I wonder if it's for a television show,"

Ben mused. "Or maybe she's going to be in a movie."

Penny arched one of her eyebrows. "You two really believe she was acting?"

"What else would it have been?" Scooter scratched his head.

"A real phone call, not make believe. I'd hate to have been the person on the other end of the line." Penny looked around the room in astonishment. "It seems like everyone in here is a Cassie Newton fan."

"Not everyone," I said. "I've only watched her show once."

"I've never even seen it." Penny chuckled when both Ben and Scooter gasped. "What's it like, anyway?"

"It's pretty much a cross between *Let's Make a Deal* and *Jeopardy*," I said.

"*Let's Make a Deal* is the game show where people wear costumes, right?" Penny asked.

"Uh-huh," I said. "Actually,

Triviamania contestants wear costumes too. But, instead of trying to win a new refrigerator or vacation like they do on that show, on *Triviamania* the contestants are in it for bragging rights alone."

Penny tucked a strand of her long blonde hair behind her ear. "You mean there're no prizes? Not even cash?"

"Nope. They only want to prove how smart they are," Scooter said. "Not everything is about money."

"You should audition for the show. You're smart," Ben said to Scooter. "It films in Chicago. We could take a road trip up there."

While the two of them discussed a boys' trip to the Windy City and what costumes they would wear, Alejandra slipped into the chair next to me. "Sorry, I'm late. Things are crazy at the nail salon."

"You must be getting excited about the grand opening," I said.

"Scared is more like it." The young woman ran her fingers through her dark hair. Normally, she was perfectly groomed—sleek hair, flawless make-up, and, of course, a perfect manicure. Except tonight, her mascara was smudged, her hair was unruly, and her nail polish was chipped. "I'll be glad when it's over. If I ever say that I want to start my own business again, shoot me."

"Running a business is tough," Penny said. "I felt the same way when I started my sailing school, and again when I took over the boat brokerage. But things got better, and they will for you too, sugar."

"I sure hope you're right," Alejandra said. "Problems keep cropping up left and right. Deliveries are late, I've got a plumbing issue, and, to top it off, one of the nail technicians I hired bailed on me, saying she got a better job offer."

"Shouldn't the landlord take care of

the plumbing issue?" Penny asked.

"I can't get a hold of him. It's like he disappeared off the face of the earth. My dad is going to take a look at it tomorrow. I would have asked Kyle to do it, but …" Alejandra's voice cracked. "But he's done a disappearing act too."

Ben leaned forward. "Did I hear that right? Mr. Wonderful isn't around anymore?"

"He broke up with me," Alejandra said.

"Good riddance," Ben muttered.

I kicked him under the table. Despite the fact Alejandra had made it clear that she only saw Ben as a good friend, he still held out hope that one day she'd agree to go out with him. When Kyle had breezed into town a few weeks ago and swept Alejandra off her feet, Ben had become resentful.

"Knock it off," I said to him before turning to Alejandra. "What happened?"

"My parents wanted to meet him, so they invited him over to dinner earlier this week. Everything went great. He bonded with my dad over baseball, brought flowers for my mom, and even ate three helpings of her enchiladas." Alejandra had a far-off look in her eyes. "That's the best way to win my mom over—praise her cooking and eat lots of it."

"Hey, I've eaten three helpings of your mom's enchiladas before," Ben said. "Heck, I could probably eat four."

I tried to kick Ben under the table again, but he pulled his leg back just in time.

"Sounds like it went well," Penny said.

"It did. Even my parents' dog loved him. Then, after dinner, Kyle and my brother went into the garage to look at this car Miguel has been working on. I was helping my mom do the dishes when I heard the two of them arguing. I went out there to see what was going on and I saw Kyle speeding away. When I asked Miguel what happened, he muttered something about my boyfriend being a jerk. Then he stormed back in the house. He threw the flowers Kyle had given my mom in the trash before telling me never to see Kyle again."

"What were they arguing about?" I asked.

"I don't know," Alejandra said. "Miguel won't talk about it. Then I got a text from Kyle saying that he couldn't see me anymore, because he was leaving town."

"Do you think that Miguel made him send that text?" Penny asked. "You've always said that he takes his role as your big brother too seriously and tries to scare off your dates."

I nodded. "Good point. It was probably because of what Miguel said to him. Besides, saying you can't see someone anymore is different than breaking up with someone."

Ben leaned back in his chair. "Sounds

like a break-up to me."

"Ben's right. He broke up with me." Alejandra's shoulders slumped. "I knew it was too good to be true. I haven't been able to sleep since then. I keep playing everything over and over in my head, trying to figure out what went wrong. And it couldn't have happened at a worse time. I've got so much to do to get the nail salon ready for the grand opening on Monday. Kyle said he'd help me, but ..."

Her eyes started to water, and I squeezed her hand. "You have friends. We can help. Scooter and I can come to the salon tomorrow to pitch in."

Alejandra leaned forward. "Are you sure?"

"Absolutely," Scooter said.

"Count me in," Penny added.

Ben grinned at Alejandra. "I'll be there too."

"Thanks, guys." She twisted a lock of her hair. "I haven't had much time to prep for tonight and I'm having a hard time concentrating. Hopefully, I won't let you down."

"It's just a silly game," I said.

Scooter shot me a look, then smiled at Alejandra. "With everything going on, we're just glad you could make it."

Alejandra looked around the room. "How come it hasn't started yet? I thought I was late."

"Oh, you missed a bit of drama," Penny said. "Cassie Newton made a surprise appearance. We're just waiting for her to come back on stage."

"I see her over there," Scooter said, pointing at the kitchen entrance. "Looks like she's talking with someone."

"It seems like quite an intense discussion," Penny said. "Do you think that guy is who she was on the phone with before?"

I turned around in my chair. The way he was positioned, I couldn't see his face. Despite that the dark buzz cut and tall frame with broad shoulders seemed familiar.

Cassie was thrusting a large red-and-white striped envelope at him. He took a step backward and held his hands up. She waved the envelope toward him, gesturing anxiously. Finally, she shoved it in the pocket of his suit jacket, then spun around and walked back into the kitchen.

The man started to follow Cassie, then changed his mind and walked in our direction.

When he passed our table, Ben said, "Hey, isn't that Kyle?"

Alejandra looked up from her phone and did a double take. She leaped to her feet and grabbed his elbow. "I've been trying to get a hold of you. We need to talk."

He paused, locked his gaze with hers for a beat, then pulled his arm away and strode toward the exit without responding.

Alejandra burst into tears and ran after him. The rest of us exchanged glances as an awkward silence fell over the table.

"What exactly do we know about Kyle?" Penny asked after a few moments.

"He's a jerk," Ben said.

"Agreed," Penny said. "But that's all we know, isn't it? We don't know where he's from, what he does for a living, or why he's in Coconut Cove."

"He is a mystery man," I said. "But we do know one thing for sure. He and Cassie Newton are acquainted. It makes you wonder what's in that envelope, doesn't it?"

CHAPTER 2
FELINE ETHICS

The next morning, Scooter and I sat in the cockpit of our sailboat, *Marjorie Jane*, watching the sunrise. The morning was relatively cool by Florida standards, so I was grateful for the warmth of Mrs. Moto's body as she snuggled on my lap.

"Do you think they're ready yet?" I asked Scooter.

The smell of warm chocolate wafted out of the galley and into the cockpit, causing my stomach to growl. Penelope

Pringle, the owner of the local bakery, the Sugar Shack, had recently begun selling pre-made pastries which you could bake at home. I was looking forward to sampling the chocolate croissants fresh from our oven.

Scooter scratched our calico behind her ears, then gave me a kiss on the forehead. "I'll go down and check on them."

After a few minutes, he returned bearing a tray of flaky croissants and fresh coffee, which he set on the bench seat next to me. Mrs. Moto stirred, bent her head down to sniff the pastries, then yowled with disappointment when she realized that they weren't stuffed with tuna.

"Hang on a minute. I've got something for you as well," he said, pulling a foil bag out of his pocket. After feeding her a few cat treats, he picked up a croissant, took a bite, and moaned in appreciation.

"They're good, aren't they?" I polished mine off, then took a sip of coffee. "The perfect way to celebrate last night's victory."

Scooter grinned. "It's hard to believe that we made it through to the finals."

"I can't believe you knew the answer to that physics question," I said.

"Just a lucky guess," Scooter said with a shrug.

"Knowing that the Banoffee Effect has to do with moving fluids? I think it would take far more than a lucky guess to get that one right."

"I think you mean the Bernoulli Effect. Banoffee is a pie with bananas, cream, and toffee."

"Close enough. Cream is a moving fluid."

"Actually, it's Cassie Newton who is the real physics whiz," he said with a dreamy look in his dark brown eyes. "She got her PhD in physics from Harvard. She had all sorts of universities vying to hire her as a professor, but then television came calling and the rest is history."

"How do you know all that?"

"I'm reading her autobiography," he said, pointing at a book lying atop one of the cockpit cushions. "It's fascinating. Did you know that she was born in Guam? And did you know that there's no sand on Guam? The beaches are covered in coral."

"No, I didn't know either of those scintillating facts."

"And did you know that she has over six hundred pairs of tennis shoes?"

"Nope, didn't know that either." I cocked my head to one side. "Why so many?"

Scooter looked at me incredulously. "That's her trademark. She has tennis shoes custom made with different themes. Didn't you notice the ones she was wearing yesterday? They had ice pops embroidered on them in honor of

Popsicle Day."

"Popsicle Day? Is that a thing?"

"You really should read her book. I'll lend it to you when I'm done." He paused, then added, "Actually, on second thought, let's check a copy out of the library for you instead."

"Why can't I read your copy?"

"You eat peanut butter."

"What does that have to do with anything?"

"You know how you are when you eat a PB&J, my little Sticky Fingers."

"Sticky Fingers?" I shook my head. "Please tell me that isn't going to be your new pet name for me."

Scooter gazed off in the distance at the boats bobbing on their mooring balls while repeating 'Sticky Fingers' to himself a few times. Then he looked back at me. "Nope. I don't think that's it. I still need to figure something out though."

"Well, it can't be worse than the last

one you gave me. I don't know why you thought a dinosaur-related name was such a good idea."

"It was cute," he said.

"Mrs. Moto is cute, especially when she's trying to play your ukulele. Calling me your Little Stegosaurus, not so much." I stood and brushed pastry flakes off my shirt. "Where did she go, anyway?"

"She's probably running around somewhere on the dock, terrorizing the seagulls."

"Those poor birds." As I looked for our wayward cat, I noticed a blue trawler in the slip next to us. "When did that boat get there?"

"Do you mean *Factoid*? It was there when we got back from the Tipsy Pirate last night."

"Really? I didn't notice it."

"Probably too caught up in the fact that the Barnacle Babes Brigade got through to the finals."

"Well, I'm not thrilled about that, but what I really couldn't stop thinking about was how Kyle treated Alejandra. She deserves better."

"She certainly does," Scooter said. "But maybe there's a rational explanation."

I raised my eyebrows. "A rational explanation for being a total jerk? Not likely."

"Her brother might have scared him off."

"It's not like Kyle is some sort of weakling. He's a big guy. I'm sure he could have stood up to Miguel if he had wanted to."

"Maybe he heard about Miguel's reputation."

"What reputation?"

"Ben told me that Miguel got into serious trouble back in high school." Scooter frowned. "The other guy ended up in the hospital."

My jaw dropped. "Wow. Alejandra

never mentioned that."

"Probably not something she likes talking about." He took his glasses off and inspected them for smudges, then looked at me. "Oh, I forgot to tell you. Mrs. Moto got some fan mail yesterday."

"Fan mail? Like she needs that. She already has a super-sized ego as it is now that you've made her an internet star." I smiled as I thought of the YouTube channel Scooter had started, which featured our cat. In addition to being popular in North America and Europe, she had a surprising number of followers in Mongolia of all places.

"The ego comes with the territory. She is a cat after all." As he climbed down the ladder into the cabin below, he said, "Wait until you see this. You're going to love it."

I leaned over the side of the boat and called Mrs. Moto. "Here, kitty-kitty. Come see what you got in the mail."

She ignored me, her attention

completely focused on a small lizard running around in front of her. It darted up one of the lines running from the neighboring boat, *Factoid*, to a cleat on the dock. I watched in horror as Mrs. Moto pursued it. Most of the people at the marina adored our cat and loved it when she came aboard their boats to visit. Though I didn't know who the owner of the blue trawler was and whether they were a cat-lover or not.

The door to the pilothouse was ajar. The lizard scurried in, followed closely by Mrs. Moto. The curtains were drawn on the pilothouse's windows so I couldn't see what was transpiring inside, but I could imagine the pouncing that was going on. Hopefully, Mrs. Moto didn't break anything in the process.

I held my breath when I saw a furry paw snake behind one of the curtains. Having seen this maneuver before, I knew that it didn't usually end well. Sadly, I was right. The curtains came crashing down revealing Mrs. Moto in mid-air. After landing gracefully on all four paws, she grabbed her prey in her mouth, then ran back to *Marjorie Jane*.

"You're a naughty cat," I said as she hopped on board our boat. I pointed at the trawler. "See what you did to their curtains?"

Mrs. Moto dropped what she was holding in her mouth, then meowed at me inquisitively, as if to say, "Weren't you impressed with my acrobatics and hunting skills?"

I shook my head at her, then turned to look back at the other boat. A couple was standing in the pilothouse, locked in a passionate embrace. The woman's hands were twined through the man's long blond hair while his hands were roaming down her back. They seemed completely unaware that there weren't any curtains shielding them from view.

After a moment, the man stepped back, revealing the woman he was with.

I gasped when I saw who it was, Cassie Newton. Still looking exceptionally well-preserved even at this early hour. The obviously much younger man stroked her cheek while he whispered something in her ear. Then he exited the pilothouse, walked out onto *Factoid's* deck, and jumped onto the dock.

I watched him saunter away, then looked back at the trawler. The curtains had been hung back up, leaving me to wonder if Cassie knew that she had been observed.

"Was getting that lizard worth it?" I asked Mrs. Moto. "I'm not sure we've made a good impression on our new boat neighbors."

The calico yowled, then nudged her prey in my direction.

"Hey, this isn't a lizard. It looks like part of an envelope." I smoothed out the crumpled up piece of blue paper, which was slightly damp with cat drool. "I wonder who Trevor is," I mused before waving the paper in front of Mrs. Moto. "You shouldn't go onto stranger's boats and steal things."

Her only response was to yawn, then clean behind her ears. Cat ethics differed greatly from human ethics. To be honest, a crumpled up paper was fair game in her books.

I tucked the envelope under the tray on the bench so that it wouldn't blow away in the breeze, then gently admonished her again. "Naughty cat."

"Who's a naughty cat?" Scooter asked as he climbed back into the cockpit. He handed me a small cardboard box, then picked up Mrs. Moto.

"She is," I said with a smile. "She went on board *Factoid*. You're not going to believe whose boat it is."

"Someone we know?"

"Only your favorite television host."

"Cassie …Cassie …" he spluttered. "Cassie Newton is docked next to us?"

His face was pale, his hands were trembling, and I was concerned that he might faint. He usually looked like this whenever there was a dead body involved. Who knew that the presence of his celebrity crush nearby could have the same effect?

"Why don't you sit down? Let's get you another croissant. The chocolate will make you feel better."

He slumped onto the bench and leaned against one of the cushions. "Did you talk to her? Should we bring her something? Some sort of welcome gift? What do you think she'd like? What do you even get a TV star? What do you think—"

I put my fingers against his lips. "Take a deep breath. No, I didn't say hi. It would have been a little awkward."

"Awkward? Why?"

"She was in the middle of something." Scooter looked at me quizzically. "She was saying goodbye to someone ...

um ... well, let's just say that it was a rather passionate farewell."

He raised his eyebrows, then grabbed a croissant. In between bites, he said, "I wonder what her husband is like. It must be great to be married to such a smart woman."

I gave Scooter a sideways look.

"And I should know, because I'm married to one myself," he said hastily.

"Not your smoothest recovery." I smiled as his face turned bright red, then took pity on him and changed the subject. "What's in the box?"

He removed the lid from the box and pulled out a tiny purple and green costume.

Mrs. Moto bounded over, sniffed the costume, then promptly jumped into the box.

"Is that what I think it is?" I asked.

"Uh-huh." He extracted the calico from the box, then pulled the costume over her head. After fastening the snaps, he grinned. "Ta-da! Our little dragon."

"Wow, the attention to detail is amazing. Look at those scales."

"One of the ladies in her fan club made it."

"That's one die-hard fan," I said.

"She and a few of her friends are RVers. They come down every winter. She's talking about coming out to the marina to meet Mrs. Moto personally."

"I hope they don't plan on her signing autographs. Her lack of opposable thumbs might make that a bit difficult."

"She could stamp her paw print instead," he said, adjusting the dragon tail while she squirmed in his arms.

When he released her, she jumped out of the cockpit and started prancing along *Marjorie Jane's* deck, showing off her latest costume to the seagulls.

"Who is this cutie-pie?" I heard a woman's voice ask.

I looked up and saw Cassie scratching Mrs. Moto's nose—the only part of her body accessible through her costume.

"That's Mrs. Moto. I'm one of her humans, Mollie. And this is my husband, Scooter."

Cassie waved at him and said hello. Instead of greeting her back, he cowered against the cushion, looking like he had just seen something terrifying, like an actual dragon landing on our boat. I nudged him and he stammered something that sounded like 'good morning' while avoiding eye contact with his celebrity crush.

"Didn't I see you folks at the Tipsy Pirate yesterday?" she asked.

"That's right," I said. "We're part of the Savvy Sailing Squad team."

"Congratulations on making it through to the finals. You had some tough competition." She leaned forward, resting her hands on *Marjorie Jane's* deck. "The two of you should definitely audition for *Triviamania*."

I glanced back at Scooter to see his

reaction to having a personal invite to audition for his favorite show.

"Audition?" he said, his voice cracking. "In Chicago?"

"We've actually decided to hold local ones here in Coconut Cove. We were going to announce it last night, but …" Her voice trailed off as she watched Mrs. Moto run to the bow of our boat, her dragon tail swishing back and forth.

"But what?" I prompted. "Did it have something to do with that phone call you had while you were on stage?"

"Phone call?" She pursed her lips, then smiled. "Oh, that. That was nothing. Just a bit of playacting. Anyway, maybe you all can help me get the word out about the auditions. They're going to take place next weekend. It's part of a trial. If they work well in Coconut Cove, we're talking about going on a *Triviamania* road trip and holding them all around the country."

I elbowed Scooter. "That sounds great, doesn't it?"

He stared at me blankly, as though he had lost the ability to comprehend English.

"We'll definitely be there," I said brightly.

Cassie pointed at Mrs. Moto. "Remember to wear a costume, like this cutie-pie has on."

"She'll be jealous that she doesn't get to audition," I joked.

Cassie smiled. "Actually, having people bring their pets is a wonderful idea. Hang on a minute, let me send my executive producer a text and see if we can organize that. The footage of animals in costumes would be great for the ratings."

While she tapped away at her phone, I whispered to Scooter, "What is wrong with you? All you've been able to talk about for weeks is Cassie Newton and now here she is standing in front of you."

"I don't know what to say," he said, pulling at his collar.

Before I could respond, Cassie interrupted. "Brittany is going to look into it. The auditions will be held at the waterfront park. Do you know it?"

"We know it well," I said. "That's where they hold the annual pet costume competition. Mrs. Moto won first prize last year."

"I can see why. She's adorable." Cassie's phone buzzed. "Sorry, more texts from Brittany."

"Before you go," I said. "I was wondering how you know Kyle Kaminsky."

"Kyle who?" she asked absentmindedly as she scrolled through her texts.

"Kyle Kaminsky. You were talking to him at the Tipsy Pirate last night. Tall, good-looking guy. He was wearing a dark suit."

"Doesn't sound familiar. But I do get a lot of fans coming up to me for my autograph. Maybe that's what you saw." She held up her phone. "Gotta go return some calls. Nice meeting you folks. I'll see you at the auditions, if not before."

"That was odd, don't you think?" I asked Scooter after she returned to her boat.

"What was odd?"

"Pretending not to know Kyle."

"Like she said, he's probably a fan."

"I'm not so sure about that." I grabbed another croissant and took a bite. "But what I am sure about is that these are delicious."

* * *

After polishing off the last of the chocolate croissants, Scooter and I headed to the nail salon to help Alejandra get ready for her grand opening. As we pulled into the parking lot of the Seaside Center, I glanced at Scooter. "You've never been here, have you?"

"Yes, I have." He pointed at the florist shop. "That's where I got you the bouquet for Mother's Day."

"I'm not sure having a fur-baby qualifies me as a mother, but I did love the flowers."

"I think you would have liked truffles more, but the chocolate shop was closed when I was here."

As we walked toward Alejandra's nail salon, I looked at the other stores located at the shopping center. Next to the florist was a deli, which made fresh bagels daily. Chocolate cream cheese on a poppy seed bagel was my idea of heaven. On the opposite side of the u-shaped building was a pet store known for its custom catnip blends—Mrs. Moto was especially partial to their Purrtastic blend—and a bookstore. Alejandra's salon was in the center of the u-shaped building next to the chocolate shop.

In the middle was a courtyard with a tiled fountain surrounded by potted plants. People enjoyed sitting at the tables and chairs positioned around the fountain while they had something to eat, read a book, or, in Mrs. Moto's case, roll around in catnip on the brick patio.

"Actually, I think I'd like pretty much anything from any of these shops," I said as Scooter held the door to the nail salon open for me.

Alejandra pressed the palm of her hand to her chest when she saw us. "Thank you so much for coming."

"Good thing you got here," Ben said, slapping Scooter on the back. "I thought I was going to have to do all the heavy lifting by myself."

"You're young," Scooter said. "I'm sure you could have managed."

"Looks like you added a new t-shirt to your collection," I said to Ben.

He smiled as he looked down at his shirt. "I thought this one was appropriate —'Work like a captain, party like a pirate.' I'm going to help Alejandra today, then it'll be party time. My band is playing at the Tipsy Pirate tonight. You guys coming?"

Scooter shook his head. "I don't think so. We were talking about having a quiet evening in and watching a movie."

"Oh, come on … you're acting like an old man," Ben joked.

"I feel like one ever since my fiftieth," Scooter said. "I can't party like I used to."

I chuckled. "Like you ever partied."

"Hey, you haven't seen me when I go to comic book conventions with my buddies," Scooter said.

"Come over and meet my parents," Alejandra said as she guided us to the back of the salon where an older couple were speaking with Penny. "This is my father, Eduardo, and this is my mother,

Josefina."

"I think we met you at the coconut carving competition last month," Scooter said.

Josefina smiled. "We did. My son, Miguel, took first prize."

"I remember that. How he managed to get a coconut to look like a Smurf is beyond me," Scooter said with a chuckle. "Where is he? I thought he was helping out today as well."

"He went to pick up some paint," Eduardo said. "He'll be back shortly."

"I told him to bring some coffee and muffins as well." Alejandra nudged me. "He's bringing a chocolate chip one especially for you. I figure you'll work harder if you've had your caffeine and sugar."

Scooter shook his head. "She's already had two chocolate croissants this morning."

"She's talking about muffins." I put my hands on my hips. "Totally different food group. Croissants are flaky, muffins aren't."

"Only you would categorize foods by their degree of flakiness," Scooter said with a chuckle. Then he turned to Alejandra. "While we wait for our next sugar fix, where do you want us to start?"

"I thought you and Ben could bring in the spa chairs. They're in the truck out back." She lowered her voice. "Do me a favor and don't let my dad try to help. They're really heavy and he has a bad back."

"No problem," Scooter said.

"Thanks." Alejandra turned to me. "I thought you and my mom could work on painting the trim by the windows while Penny and my dad assemble the shelving units."

"Sounds like a plan," I said. "But before we get started, it looks like my second breakfast has arrived."

"Who wants coffee?" Miguel asked as

he pushed open the door. As Josefina grabbed the carrier tray from him, I looked at the young man who was the spitting image of his father—a stocky, muscular build, thick dark hair, and warm brown eyes. It was hard to reconcile the cheerful guy in front of me with the story Scooter had told me about his troubled past in high school.

"Sis, want to grab the muffins from the car?" he asked Alejandra.

We chatted about the upcoming *Triviamania* auditions while we sipped on our coffee drinks and ate our muffins. Ben was excited to wear a pirate costume, while Penny was planning on going as a mermaid. Scooter was undecided about what to wear, concerned about making the best possible impression on Cassie that he could.

Miguel crumpled up his coffee cup and tossed it in the trash. "Penelope sure knows how to bake muffins." Then he kissed his mother on the cheek. "But they don't hold a candle to your churros, mama."

She laughed as she swatted him away. "I've never seen anyone eat as many of them as you do."

"It's time we got to work," Alejandra snapped. "We have lots to do and all anyone can talk about is churros."

Everyone fell silent, startled by her uncharacteristic outburst.

"I'm sorry." Alejandra ran her fingers through her hair. "It's just the stress of everything. Opening up this salon has been my dream since I was in high school, but just look at the state of this place. There's no way I'll be ready for the grand opening on Monday. I'm a failure."

Josefina put her arm around her daughter's shoulders and murmured something to her in Spanish.

Alejandra nodded, then straightened her shoulders. "You're right, mama. I can do this ... *We* can do this."

"Okay, you heard the lady," Scooter said. "Let's get to work."

Later that evening, everyone was exhausted, but we had made huge progress. The spa chairs had been installed along the far wall, manicure stations were in position, nail polishes were on display on one of the shelving units, and a cozy reception area was set up in the front of the store by the large bay window. Only a few finishing touches needed to be put in place, which Alejandra could take care of the next day on her own.

I gave my friend a hug. "It looks great. This is going to be a huge success."

"Thanks, Mollie," she said, a huge grin on her face as she surveyed her salon.

"Anyone hungry?" Josefina asked as she carried a large platter in from the back room. We all nodded enthusiastically. "Miguel, carry this outside. We can eat on the patio.

Eduardo, can you grab the sodas from the fridge?"

After we gathered outside, she peeled off the tinfoil from the platter.

"Are those tamales?" Scooter asked.

"Almost as good as her churros," Miguel said as he handed them out.

After peeling the corn husk back on mine and taking a bite, I sighed with contentment. "Ooh, that beef is delicious."

"You should try the chicken ones," Penny said. "They have olives in them."

Josefina beamed as everyone praised her cooking. While we relaxed and ate our dinner, a silver Mercedes Benz pulled into the parking lot. An older man who was dressed like he had just golfed eighteen holes at an exclusive country club got out. He looked at his watch, then reached into the car and grabbed a briefcase.

"Anybody know who that is?" Ben asked.

"Never seen him or that car around before," Penny said. "Must not be a local."

We watched as he walked into the florist shop. "Maybe he got in trouble with the missus and is getting some flowers to make it up to her," Ben joked.

When he walked out a few minutes later with only his briefcase in hand, Scooter said, "I guess he realized that chocolate is the way to a woman's heart."

"Nope," Alejandra said. "Looks like he's going into the deli. Bagels will do it every time."

As Josefina passed around cookies, the man emerged from the deli, again with only his briefcase in sight.

"I guess he can't make up his mind," I said.

He glanced inside the nail salon, then walked past it into the Himalayan Highlands chocolate shop. Our table was right across from it, so we had a bird's-eye view. The owner, Angus Tanaka, greeted the older gentleman warmly and pointed at the truffles in the display cases. The man set his briefcase on the counter, opened it up, and handed Angus an envelope.

The expression on Angus' face as he read the letter inside shifted from surprise to confusion, and then to anger. He jabbed his finger at the man, yelling at him. The man shrugged, snapped his briefcase shut and walked next door to the pet store, followed by the bookstore, where he repeated the same pattern—going inside for a few minutes and leaving empty-handed.

Finally, he walked toward us. "Do any of you know where I can find Alejandra Lopez?"

"That's me," she said, wiping her hands on her jeans. "What can I do for you?"

"It's about your lease," he said.

Alejandra furrowed her brow. "If you're

interested in leasing space here, you should speak with Mr. Owens. He owns the shopping center."

"He used to. I'm the new owner." He held out his hand, the heavy gold bracelet on his wrist glinting under the overhead light. "Sorry, I should have introduced myself. Robert Ronaldo."

"Oh, I didn't realize that Mr. Owens was selling. He never mentioned anything about it. I suppose that's why he was hard to get a hold of when I had a plumbing issue." She laughed. "I guess you're the guy I go to now when something comes up."

He stared at her impassively. "Not really."

"Huh?"

"I'm terminating your lease. I have a new tenant taking over the space at the end of next month."

Alejandra's jaw dropped. "But that's not possible. I signed a two-year lease with an option to renew for another three years at the end of the first year. My grand opening is on Monday."

"It's Saturday today, so that gives you time to cancel it," he said coolly.

"You don't understand," she said, wringing her hands together. "Opening this nail salon is my dream. I've worked so hard for it. You can't take it away from me."

"You're young. You'll have other dreams." He opened his briefcase, pulled out an envelope and thrust it in her hands. "If you have any questions, you can contact my attorney. His details are listed inside." Then he walked toward his car, swinging his briefcase back and forth while humming to himself.

CHAPTER 3
THE PROBLEM WITH BOWLING SHOES

Miguel stared at Robert Ronaldo's retreating back for a moment, his fists tightly clenched, then jogged toward him. The older man pressed his key fob to unlock his car, but before he could open the door, Miguel grabbed his shoulder and spun him around. I couldn't hear what he said to the older man, but his body language was clear— mess with my sister and I'll mess with you.

Robert Ronaldo said something which caused Miguel to take a few steps backward, holding up his hands as though he was surrendering. The new owner of the Seaside Center got into his car and started the engine. As he reversed out of his parking spot, Miguel dashed toward his own car.

Eduardo yelled after him, "Where are you going, *mijo*?"

"I have to take care of something," Miguel said over his shoulder before getting into his car.

Josefina made the sign of the cross as Miguel sped after the Mercedes Benz. She turned to her husband and began speaking to him in Spanish. I couldn't understand what she was saying, but it was clear that she was agitated.

Alejandra placed a hand on her mother's arm and started to say something to her, but was interrupted when Angus Tanaka approached waving an envelope.

"Did you get one of these too?" His face was flushed with anger, almost matching his fiery red hair.

Alejandra held up her envelope, a slack expression on her face. "What are we going to do?"

"We're going to fight it, that's what we're going to do," he said, his nostrils flaring. "My family has had a chocolate shop at the Seaside Center since I was a boy. There's no way some rich dude can just waltz in here and tell me to take a hike. I'll stop him no matter what it takes."

"Do you mind if I look at one of those letters?" Scooter asked.

The chocolate shop owner shrugged and handed his to Scooter. Then he looked over at where I was standing. "Mollie, is that you?"

"Uh-huh. And this is my husband, Scooter. Scooter, this is Angus Tanaka."

As the two of them shook hands, Scooter said, "My wife is probably your best customer."

"She is … I mean she was …" He ran his fingers through his hair. "No, she *is* my best customer," he said emphatically. "And she's going to stay that way, because I'm not moving my shop from this location. Do you know how hard it is to find retail space to lease in Coconut Cove?"

"It's nearly impossible." Alejandra chewed on her lip for a moment. "I spent months looking for a place for my nail salon."

"I don't understand why he's doing this," I said. "He already has good tenants. Why would he want to drive them out?"

"It could be that he's looking for a different type of tenant." Scooter pursed his lips as he finished examining Angus' letter. He folded it up and passed it back to him. "This all looks legit."

"What do you mean by a different kind of tenant?" Alejandra asked.

"I heard of something similar happening in Ocean Springs. They've driven local businesses out and brought in chain stores to take their place."

"But wouldn't that be against zoning?" Ben asked.

Scooter shook his head. "This place is already zoned for commercial businesses. I doubt that there are any restrictions on whether the businesses should be local or not."

Penny folded her arms across her chest. "I know that I'm a transplant from Texas, but Coconut Cove is my home. One of the things I love about this place is its small-town feel, and a large part of that is due to the local shops."

"Yeah, what she said," a deep voice said beside me. I turned and saw the owner of the bookstore clutching an envelope in his beefy hand. "Keep Coconut Cove local."

Standing next to him was the young couple who owned the pet store. "Keep

Coconut Cove local," they said in unison. The owners of the other stores in the shopping center had gathered around us and joined in, chanting, "Keep Coconut Cove local! Keep Coconut Cove local!"

"Strike, strike!" Ben yelled. A few people started to join in, but their voices trailed off when Scooter held up his hands.

"Folks, I don't think a strike fits the situation. You don't work for Mr. Ronaldo. You lease space from him. If you stop working, that only hurts your bottom line, not his."

"Well then, what do we do?" Alejandra asked.

"You could stage a protest," I suggested.

Ben put his hands around his mouth like a megaphone and yelled, "Protest! Protest!"

The crowd joined in, chanting until they ran out of steam. Then the owner of the florist shop raised her hand meekly. "How exactly do we protest?"

"We need to get Anabel Dalton on the case," I said. "She's practically a professional protester. You all remember the protest she organized to stop cuts to library funding, right?" Everyone nodded. "How about the protest against not allowing unicycles on the bike path?" A few people started clapping. "And what about earlier this year at the bowling alley when she—"

Ben interrupted. "What's there to protest about bowling?"

"The shoes," I said, surprised that it needed to be said out loud. "They're hideous and smell bad. Anabel Dalton had the courage to stand up for the rights of our feet."

A few people furrowed their brows at this explanation. Clearly, they weren't bowlers. Then Angus hopped onto one of the chairs and led the group in chanting, "Protest, protest!"

The chant died down when Josefina passed around more of her delicious cookies. It's hard to sound the war cry when your mouth is full of crumbly shortbread.

"So, what's the plan?" Alejandra asked.

"Who's our leader?" another woman chimed in.

"Scooter, Scooter, Scooter!" Ben yelled.

Most of the crowd joined in, but I did hear a few people murmur to each other, "Who's Scooter?"

Scooter's eyes grew wide as Ben pointed at him and continued chanting. Finally, Scooter held up his hands and motioned to the crowd to quiet down. "I appreciate Ben suggesting that I help, but I don't own a shop here. One of you should lead the protest."

Ben put his arm around Scooter's shoulder. "No way, man. You're a natural leader. You own your own telekinesis business—"

"Telecommunications, not telekinesis," Scooter corrected.

"That has to do with phones, right?" After my husband nodded, Ben turned to the crowd. "This man manages projects all the time. And he's really good with spreadsheets."

"Spreadsheets," the florist said in awe. "Spreadsheets confuse me."

"And he's a lawyer."

Scooter frowned. "I'm not a lawyer."

"But you know a lawyer, right?"

"Yes, I do," Scooter said cautiously.

"Great." Ben slapped Scooter on the back. "You can organize the protest and check with a lawyer about this Ronaldo guy's letters."

A voice piped up in the back. "Scooter, Scooter, Scooter!" The rest of the shop owners joined in. Once their voices had grown hoarse and they had polished off the last of the cookies, they thanked Scooter for taking on the role of the

Seaside Center Protest Committee Chair.

After they went back to their shops, Scooter put his head in his hands and groaned. "Why me?"

I squeezed his arm. "I think it's a compliment."

He looked at me wearily. "A compliment is when you tell someone you like their tie. This is … not that."

Ben walked over to us. "I spoke with everyone. We've agreed to have our first committee meeting at the Tipsy Pirate tomorrow afternoon."

"The drinks better be on you, Ben," Scooter said.

"Me?" Ben asked innocently.

While the two of them debated about who would be buying the first round, I watched as Miguel drove back into the parking lot. As he got out of his car, I heard his father ask him where he had been.

"I was taking care of things," Miguel

said.

"What does that mean, *mijo*?" Eduardo asked.

Miguel shrugged. "It's better you don't know. Let's just leave it at that."

* * *

"Are you sure you want to do this?" Scooter asked me as we were driving down Main Street the next morning.

"It was my idea," I said.

"Yeah, but taking *Marjorie Jane* to the Bahamas is kind of a big deal." He glanced over at me. "I know that this whole sailing thing was my idea originally, so I just want to be sure that you're on board with it."

"I'm definitely not committing to sailing around the world like you'd love to do, but I am up for going to the Bahamas for a few months and seeing how it goes."

Scooter stopped to let some tourists cross the street, then reached over and squeezed my hand. "You're my best girl."

"Don't let Mrs. Moto hear you say that." I glanced at the rear seat where the calico was curled up. "She thinks she's your best girl."

He chuckled, then pointed at Penelope's Sugar Shack. "I suppose you'll want a coffee before we run our errands."

"Definitely. I'm going to need a caffeine jolt to deal with shopping for boat parts."

As he pulled into the bakery's parking lot, Scooter sighed. "I might need a coffee too. I was up all night thinking about everything we have to do to get the boat ready to leave for the Bahamas. And I'm still not sure what's wrong with *Marjorie Jane's* anchor light. Hopefully, it just needs a new bulb."

"If it is the bulb, how do we fix that?"

"Someone climbs up to the top of the mast and changes it."

"The top of the mast?" I gulped. "That's a long way up there. It sounds dangerous."

Scooter patted my hand. "Don't worry, I'll take care of it."

"But how? Do you use a giant ladder?"

"No. You sit in what's called a 'bosun's chair' and someone hoists you up using the line that runs from the top of the mast—"

The sound of a yapping dog interrupted him. Mrs. Moto jumped up onto my shoulder and pressed her face against the window. I opened the door and was greeted by not one, but two overly enthusiastic Yorkshire terriers.

"Look, it's Frick and Frack," I said to the calico, but she was already on the ground saying hello to her canine friends. "I wonder who they're here with —Anabel or Chief Dalton?"

"Looks like both of them," Scooter said, pointing at the bakery.

"Are they holding hands?" I asked,

staring at the chief of police and his ex-wife through the window. "I knew the two of them were getting back together. I wonder how he's going to propose to her this time."

"Propose?" Scooter grinned. "I think you might be getting a little ahead of yourself."

"I'm not so sure. The chief is still trimming those bushy eyebrows of his. That's a sure sign that he's smitten with her. Anyway, I'm glad they're both here. We can kill two birds with one stone."

"I know we need to talk with Anabel about the protest, but what do you need to speak with the chief about? Please tell me it doesn't have anything to do with starting a neighborhood UFO watch. Remember what happened last time you pitched that idea to him?"

"Don't worry. It has nothing to do with that." I scooped up Mrs. Moto, pushed the door open, then greeted Anabel and the chief. "Good morning. Fancy seeing the two of you here."

The burly man looked over his shoulder at me, then abruptly released Anabel's hand. "Mrs. McGhie," he said formally. Then he nodded at Scooter. "Mr. McGhie."

Anabel was less formal, enveloping Mrs. Moto and me in a hug before giving Scooter a peck on the cheek. "Tiny has the day off," she said, glancing at her ex. "We're going to take the dogs to the park."

"Will you still be able to make it to the protest meeting at the Tipsy Pirate this afternoon?" I asked.

The chief's posture stiffened. "Protest?"

"The new owner of the Seaside Center is trying to oust all the local business owners and replace them with generic chain stores," Anabel said. "We're protesting to keep Coconut Cove local. I told you all about it last night when we were at the movies."

I pointed back and forth between the two of them. "You guys were together last night and now again this morning? Pretty cozy."

"Mrs. McGhie, how I spend my free time and who I spend it with is none of your business," the chief said brusquely.

"Don't mind, Tiny," Anabel said, looping her hand through his arm. "He has a lot on his mind."

"The speed trap not bringing in enough revenue?" I asked.

"We don't have a speed trap," the chief said gruffly.

"Sure you do. It's on the main road as you come into town. Everybody knows about it."

Chief Dalton stared at me impassively for a few moments, then turned to Scooter. "Did you watch the game last night?"

While the guys talked sports, Anabel told me what was really concerning the chief. "The receptionist at the police station quit without notice. It's been chaos down there ever since. No one knows how to operate the phones, the filing system is a mess, and they found a mud dauber nest in the break room."

"Mud daubers?"

"Those wasps that build their nests from mud. You must have seen them around. They're basically harmless."

"Wasps? There's no such thing as a harmless wasp. I hate wasps." I shuddered. "I can see why the chief is in such a bad mood."

"Yeah, and if that wasn't bad enough, apparently, there's a private investigator in town. Tiny hates private investigators." She pulled out her wallet, paying for her and the chief's coffee drinks. "One of his buddies up north told him that there's someone on his turf doing a fraud investigation. Tiny is furious that someone is nosing around in his jurisdiction. He thinks they should have had the professional courtesy to check in with him first."

After I placed our order—extra chocolaty mocha for me and a vanilla latte for Scooter—I grabbed some napkins. "Hmm … private investigator. Maybe I should look into becoming one of those."

"Ahem," the chief said behind me. "What's this about becoming a private investigator, Mrs. McGhie? You realize that you need a license, don't you?"

"I already have one."

"No, I don't mean a driver's license."

"That's not what I meant either." I reached into my purse, pulled out a green leather badge holder, and flipped it open so that he could see my credentials.

As he examined it, he suppressed a smile. "I didn't mean one issued by the Federation for … what does FAROUT stand for again?"

"The Federation for Alien Research, Outreach, and UFO Tracking. I'm a fully accredited and *licensed* investigative reporter."

He handed me back my badge. "Anyone can get one of these made."

"Not with the official FAROUT logo, they can't," I said. "But I'm glad you brought up the subject."

The chief frowned. "What subject?"

"Having you speak at—"

Scooter handed me my mocha. "Don't you think we should get going?"

"In a minute," I said. "I've been trying to get a hold of the chief all week. Now that I have his undivided attention, it's the perfect opportunity to make the arrangements."

"Arrangements for what?" the chief asked dryly.

"Your speech at the next FAROUT meeting."

"I never agreed to do that."

"Of course you did."

"No, I didn't."

"I sent you an email."

"You send me lots of emails," he said, shaking his head. "I don't have time to read all of them."

"Well, this one was marked important. It had the suggested talking points for your speech too. In it, I also said that if you couldn't make the meeting to let me know. You never emailed back to say that you couldn't be there, so that means you agreed to it."

The chief's face reddened as his neatly trimmed eyebrows twitched. He squeezed his coffee cup so hard that I thought the contents would spill out. "Just because I never emailed you back doesn't mean I'm going to come speak at your meeting."

Anabel placed her hand on his arm and made soothing noises. "Actually, Tiny, I think it's a great idea."

"You do?"

"Uh-huh. It's good for the chief of police to have outreach events within the community. I was planning on being at the meeting. I'd love to hear you speak at it."

"You would?"

She nodded. "I would."

He rubbed his chin. "Well, in that case —"

"Great, it's settled." I grinned. "I'll resend the email with all the details."

* * *

Later that afternoon, Scooter stood at the head of a long table in the Tipsy Pirate. "Can I have everyone's attention, please?" Seated around the table were the tenants of the Seaside Center and their supporters, including Ben, Penny, and Anabel. The group was chatting enthusiastically with each other, eager to plan the protest against Robert Ronaldo and his bid to strip Coconut Cove of its local character.

As I looked around the bar, I noted the usual mix of tourists and locals. The former group was in awe of the kitschy decor, clamoring to take selfies in front of the wooden statue of the famous pirate and local legend, Coconut Carl, while drinking shots of rum. A baseball game was playing on the televisions scattered around the bar, and the crowd erupted into cheers as one of the players slid into home base to tie the game.

Scooter rapped his knuckles on the table, struggling to be heard over the din. "Folks, can I get your attention?"

"Maybe I can help," I said, then put my fingers between my lips and whistled loudly. Everyone at our table, and a few of the other tables, spun their heads away from the TV monitors and looked at me. "All yours, Scooter."

"Thanks, my little ..." he paused and looked at me. I could see the gears in his head whirring as he tried to figure out what pet name he should bestow on me this time. "Thanks, my little cinnamon stick."

I shook my head. Cinnamon was great in small doses, especially in apple pie. Though as a pet name, not so much.

"My little nutmeg? My little clove?"

I continued to shake my head. What was with all the festive spices? The holidays were months away.

"My little … well never mind, I'll figure something out later," he said to me. Then he straightened his shoulders and addressed the table. "I call the first meeting of the Seaside Center Protest Committee to order. As you can see from the agenda which I passed out, we have a lot to cover. I'll start off with an update from my lawyer friend, then I'll hand things over to Anabel Dalton to discuss the logistics for the protest."

Ben nudged Angus. "See, I told you he knew a lawyer."

"I hope it's a good one," Angus said.

Scooter cleared his throat. "I'm afraid the news from the lawyer isn't great.

Robert Ronaldo is within his rights to terminate your leases."

The owner of the bookstore slammed his fist on the table, rattling the silverware. "But my agreement was with Mr. Owens."

"Yes, but when Mr. Owens sold the shopping plaza to Mr. Ronaldo, the termination clause went into effect. I'm afraid you don't have any legal recourse. Our best option is to exert public pressure through a protest and get Mr. Ronaldo to change his mind."

"Doesn't sound like this lawyer is very good," Angus said to Ben.

The florist raised her hand. "Can we fight it in court?"

Scooter shrugged. "You can try, but that would take a lot of time and money. Sadly, there's still no guarantee that you'd be successful."

Alejandra put her head in her hands. "This can't be happening," she muttered.

"Why don't we focus on what we do have control over," Scooter suggested. "Anabel, can you talk us through the plans for the protest?"

After Anabel explained the keys to a successful protest—clear messaging, compelling visuals, and creative clothing —she suggested that the event take place on the coming Saturday.

"We always have a lot of visitors in town over Labor Day weekend," she said. "It will be a great chance to get some visibility for our cause. We could even march down Main Street where everyone would see us."

After the group murmured their agreement, she started listing things which needed to be done to prepare.

"Would you mind noting down who has been assigned to which task?" Scooter passed me his laptop. "I've set up a spreadsheet that you can use."

"I hate spreadsheets," I said.

"You'll love this one," he said. "It's

color coded."

"Making something colorful doesn't make it any more enjoyable especially a spreadsheet."

He gave me a peck on the cheek. "How about if I get you some eggrolls after the meeting as a reward?"

"Deal," I said, my fingers poised above the keyboard.

After the assignments had been handed out, and the rest of the items on the agenda had been addressed, Scooter said, "Great work, everyone. I think we're in good shape for the protest this coming weekend."

"He's very organized," Angus said to Ben.

Ben nodded. "See, I told you. He's the perfect leader for us."

"Okay, we'll meet again on Tuesday night. Before we go, does anyone have any questions?" Scooter asked. "Any other business that we need to cover today?"

"Did we ever find out anything about Robert Ronaldo?" the florist asked.

"I've got some information on him," Penny said. "I did some digging. Turns out he's a developer from Chicago. He buys shopping centers around the country, gets rid of the local business owners, and turns the space over to chain stores."

"Has any community successfully fought him in the past?" the deli owner asked.

Penny folded her hands and looked down at the table. "Unfortunately, no."

The group looked downcast, but Scooter was determined to keep everyone's motivation up. "Then we'll be the first, right?"

"Keep Coconut Cove local," Ben chanted. The rest of the group chimed in, their voices growing louder and louder as they did fist pumps in the air.

After a minute, Penny stood to get everyone's attention. "I also have one other piece of interesting information about Robert Ronaldo." She paused for dramatic effect, then said, "He's Cassie Newton's husband."

Scooter blanched. "Cassie Newton? No, that can't be right."

"It is," Penny said. "They've been married for over fifteen years."

"But … But I can't lead a protest against Cassie Newton's husband," he protested.

Scooter slumped in his chair with his head in his hands, completely aghast that he was the chair of a committee fighting his celebrity crush's husband. I wondered who it was that Cassie had been locked in a passionate embrace with, because it definitely hadn't been Robert Ronaldo.

CHAPTER 4
GREEN NAIL POLISH

The next evening, Scooter and I headed to the nail salon for the grand opening celebration.

"Pretty impressive turnout for a Monday night," Scooter said as we circled the parking lot looking for a spot. "I think half the town is here."

"It wouldn't surprise me," I said. "Alejandra was born and raised in Coconut Cove. Everyone knows how hard she worked waitressing to put herself through business classes at the community college, not to mention saving her money to open the salon. Folks want to help celebrate her success."

"That's one of the nice things about living in a small town," Scooter said. "It feels like an extended family."

"That's exactly why everyone is up in arms to fight what's happening at the shopping center. I spoke with Anabel earlier. She thinks there's going to be a huge crowd at the protest march. Once Robert Ronaldo sees how much support there is, he'll have to back down."

"I hope you're right," Scooter said. "But I still don't think I should be involved."

"Of course you should. We can't pull this off without you."

"But Robert Ronaldo is married to Cassie Newton."

"So? You just met Cassie. You don't owe her or her husband anything, even if you do have a crush on her."

"I don't have a crush on Cassie."

"Uh. Yes, you do." I laughed. "But Alejandra is our friend. In fact, she's more than that. What is it you just said about Coconut Cove being like an extended family?"

He took a deep breath. "You're right."

"I don't think we're going to find a spot here," I said as we circled the lot for the fourth time.

"You're right about that too," he said. "Let's go park across the road by the beach."

After we got the car situated in the overflow lot, we walked along the path that cut through the dense brush which bordered the beach. Once we reached the other end, we crossed the road and made our way to the shopping center.

I pointed at a sign which had been recently hung over the entrance to Alejandra's salon. "I had wondered what she was going to name it—the Nail Nook is perfect. It's a shame Ned and

Nancy couldn't be here for the party. Nancy would have really liked the name of the salon."

"This is the first time they've gone on vacation in a few years, isn't it?" Scooter asked.

"Yes, I'm surprised they felt comfortable leaving the management of the marina in other people's hands. Especially Nancy. She's such a control freak."

We greeted some friends, then grabbed some sodas. Alejandra's parents were wandering through the crowd, carrying trays laden with appetizers.

"I'm so glad you could make it," Josefina said as she offered me a bacon-wrapped date.

Scooter grabbed a pork tostada and popped it in his mouth. "Where's Alejandra?"

"She's around here somewhere." Josefina said. "I know that she's looking for you, Mollie. She has a special surprise for you."

"A surprise for me?" I asked, raising my eyebrows. "I can't believe she'd be thinking of me on her big day."

"She's probably in the salon." Josefina smiled. "Why don't you go see if you can find her."

Alejandra squealed when I stuck my head through the door. "There you are. Come meet Francine."

She led me over to a woman who was seated at one of the manicure stations. Her silver corkscrew curls stuck up at odd angles, reminding me of a Brillo pad that had given up on life after having scrubbed one too many pots. Her hot pink lipstick was smudged and her false eyelashes looked like they might slip off her eyelids at any moment.

"I was lucky to convince Francine to come work for me," Alejandra said. "She moved to Coconut Cove to spend more time with her daughter and grandchildren. Though when she heard how desperate I was after one of my nail technicians quit, she took pity on me and came out of retirement."

"Don't be silly, sweetie," Francine said. "I'm enjoying it."

"You're a lifesaver." Alejandra smiled. "This is Mollie. The friend I was telling you about."

Francine chuckled. "So, you're the crazy gal who believes in those little green men."

"I'm not crazy," I said. "There's plenty of scientific proof—"

"I'm just kidding you, sweetie," she said, interrupting me before I could share the latest studies about the number of habitable worlds in our galaxy. "Now, why don't you have a seat and we'll get started on your manicure."

"My manicure?"

"I know you're not really into getting your nails done," Alejandra said as she steered me toward the other side of the manicure station. "But this isn't going to be an ordinary manicure. Trust me, you're going to love it."

After I sat down, Francine examined my cuticles. She frowned. "This may take a while."

"Okay, I'll leave the two of you to it," Alejandra said before scooting off to greet newcomers to the party.

After Francine filed my nails, she showed me three bottles of nail polish. "Which one of these would you prefer?"

"They're all different shades of green," I said.

"Yes, that's what Alejandra suggested. She thought green would go well with the surprise she has planned for you." She leaned forward and lowered her voice. "You're a really good friend to go along with this. Personally, I would never have painted anyone's nails green back when I owned a nail salon. But you know these young people. They're all about the latest trends. How about if we go with something more classic instead, like a pale pink or even a red?"

I wasn't sure what I was more offended about—the fact that she didn't think I was young or the fact that she didn't think I could be trendy. Okay, I was a middle-aged woman, and I didn't exactly dress like I just walked off a runway, but still I wasn't completely out of touch with what was fashionable.

"Why don't we go with that one." I pointed at the middle bottle.

Francine shrugged. "If you're sure."

While she applied the bright green nail polish, she told me about the imminent arrival of her grandbaby number three. "My daughter's husband just walked out on her, she's thrilled that I live nearby and can help out with the kids."

"Is it going to be a problem working at the Nail Nook?" I asked.

"It's just part-time until she can find another manicurist. Not that she calls us manicurists." She rolled her eyes. "Nail technicians, that's what she says."

"What's the difference?"

"There isn't one in my book." She inspected my fingernails. "That looks good. Okay, now for the surprise."

I watched in amazement as she deftly added designs on top of the green nail polish using fine brushes. "Wow," I said when she was finished. "I wouldn't call you a nail technician either. I'd call you an artist. This is amazing work."

"Thank you," she smiled. "The designs are a little silly, but it's what Alejandra wanted."

"I love them," I said, holding up my hands and admiring the work.

"Let's move you under the dryer for a bit. Don't want you smudging them and ruining all my hard work."

As we walked to the front of the salon, I heard voices shouting. I knelt down on one of the chairs in the reception area and peered out the window. Robert

Ronaldo was standing in front of the shop, penned in by Miguel and Angus with the other tenants forming a circle around them.

"I wonder what he's doing here," I mused.

"Jumping sassafras," Francine said quietly behind me.

I turned to look at her. "What was that?"

She waved her hand in the air. "Just something my grandmother used to say. Come on, let's get you under the dryer, sweetie."

I reluctantly sat at the dryer, twisting my neck so that I could see the drama unfolding outside. At one point, Angus shoved his new landlord. I was worried that things might come to serious blows when Brittany Abernethy elbowed her way between the three guys. The executive producer of *Triviamania* adjusted the scarf around her neck, then pointed her finger at Angus and Miguel as if scolding them. After a brief discussion, she looked sternly at Robert Ronaldo before leading him away.

As I impatiently waited for my nails to dry, questions ran through my head that needed answering. What was the executive producer of *Triviamania* doing at the grand opening party for the Nail Nook? Was she there to meet Robert Ronaldo? Why had he made an appearance? Based on Angus and Miguel's reaction, it certainly didn't look like he had reconsidered terminating the leases.

I chewed on my lip. It looked like everything was going to depend on making the protest march such a huge success that he had no other option, but to change his mind.

* * *

"What happened?" I asked Scooter, who had come into the salon in search of me. "I saw Robert Ronaldo surrounded by the Seaside Center tenants."

"Everyone is pretty hot under the collar," he said. "Even the lady who owns the florist shop looked like she wanted to punch him."

"Why was he here, anyway?" I asked. "He already gave the tenants the letters. There's no need to come back down here and antagonize everyone."

"I heard him say that he had a voice message saying that the tenants wanted to speak with him."

"Really? Who called him?"

"No one did. At least that's what they all said."

"But what caused everyone to get so angry?"

Scooter pursed his lips. "He told them that he was planning on doing renovations to the shopping center and that he'd be closing the parking lot during them. That's what got them really up in arms."

"Understandably. That will cut down their business dramatically. People won't want to park across the street in the overflow lot."

"I think he's trying to drive them out early. According to the leases, he has to give them until the end of next month to vacate the premises, but that might not be soon enough for him."

I pulled my hands out from under the dryer and held them up for Scooter to see. "Like them?"

"Are those little spaceships?" he asked, adjusting his glasses to get a better look.

"Uh-huh. And see the ringed planet on this finger?"

"Wow, the detail is amazing. That looks just like Saturn."

"Check out my right thumb."

"She looks familiar."

"Princess Leia from *Star Wars*," I said.

"Wow. Alejandra did this?"

"No, it was a lady named Francine.

She's the new nail technician, or manicurist as she likes to call herself."

"She's very talented."

"She sure is. I can see the appeal of getting manicures regularly, assuming they all look like this." As I admired my nails, I asked Scooter to grab my phone out of my purse and take a picture for the FAROUT newsletter.

"It's not in there," he said after a few moments.

"Of course it is," I said. "Have another look."

He sighed, then began pulling out the contents of my purse and setting them on the table. "Why do you need this many markers?"

"You can never have too many markers."

"You have twenty-seven of them in your purse. That's twenty-six too many." He arched an eyebrow as he pulled the next item out. "Is this duct tape? Do I even want to know what that's for?"

"It's for emergencies."

"What kind of emergencies do you have that require twenty-seven markers, a roll of duct tape, pliers, and a ball of twine?" He shook his head as he turned my purse upside down and shook it. "Nope, your phone isn't in there."

"Can you check the side pocket?" As he pulled out a bag of silver-wrapped chocolates, I said, "And speaking of emergencies, can you pop one of those Hershey's kisses in my mouth? I don't want to smudge my nails."

"Losing your phone is an emergency?" I nodded while he unwrapped the foil from one of the chocolates. "I don't know how you can eat another bite. I had one too many of those delicious cookies Josefina baked. We've really fallen off the wagon with our diet."

"Yes, but that wagon was really uncomfortable," I said. "It was full of food that tasted like cardboard and rutabagas. The ground is paved in sugar and bacon. Ooh and chocolate."

"Good thing you're not a writer," he said. "That was a really bad analogy. Or was it a metaphor?"

"Who knows? I'd be a terrible writer," I said. "Grammar and punctuation get in the way of a good story. But maybe I do need a career change. What do you think, should I hang out the private investigator shingle?"

"No," he said decisively. "It's bad enough that you get dragged into these murder investigations. Don't go out seeking dangerous situations."

"But people would pay me."

"We're doing fine financially. We certainly don't need money badly enough for you to put your life in jeopardy." He started putting the contents back into my purse. "No phone. Do you think you left it on the boat?"

I smacked my forehead, smearing one of Saturn's rings slightly. "Oh, I know where it is—the car. I was charging it on our way over here. Let's walk back and get it. I want to take some pictures of the party before everyone leaves too."

As we walked back along the path through the brush, Scooter stopped me. "Hang on a minute. I have a rock in my shoe."

As he bent down to remove his shoe, a shot rang out. He looked up at me, his lips trembling. "Was that a gun shot?"

"I think so. Call 911. Someone could be hurt."

As he grabbed his phone out of his pocket, I darted down the path. "I'm going to see if anyone needs help," I shouted back over my shoulder.

"Mollie, hang on. It could be dangerous," Scooter yelled after me.

Halfway down the path, I tripped over an open briefcase, landing on the ground. As I rose to my feet, I noticed file folders, loose papers, a small white box, and pens strewn to the right of me.

Brushing sand off my clothes, I looked to my left, then recoiled in horror when I saw a body lying on the ground in a pool of blood.

Someone had shot Robert Ronaldo. And, from the looks of it, it had been fatal.

CHAPTER 5
APPLE VS. PEACH PIE

"It's all my fault," Penny said, as she paced back and forth on the patio in front of the nail salon.

The ambulance had left—the absence of lights and sirens a clear indicator that Robert Ronaldo hadn't survived. The police had secured the crime scene. Chief Dalton and his officers were busy speaking to everyone that had been at the grand opening party when the shooting occurred.

When Penny had seen Scooter and I

walking up to the nail salon—a pained expression on our faces—she waved us over. Now, she ran her fingers through her long blonde hair while repeating over and over how it was all her fault.

Scooter gave me a sideways look as he pulled a chair out from one of the tables for her.

"What's your fault?" I asked, sitting in the chair next to her.

She took a deep breath, then fixed her gaze on me. "Chief Dalton overheard me telling Ben that I thought Miguel might have a gun."

I gasped. "Miguel has a gun?"

"Might have," she said. "My Spanish is a little rusty."

I furrowed my brow. "Your Spanish?"

"Do you remember when we were helping Alejandra get her shop ready on Saturday and Miguel got in his car and sped off after Robert Ronaldo?" We both nodded. "Well, I overheard Josefina and Eduardo talking. I could swear that they said something about Miguel having a gun. His mother was worried that there would be a repeat of the trouble he had in high school." She chewed on her lip for a moment. "At least that's what I think they said."

"Why were you telling Ben about it?" Scooter asked

"Well, we all saw the ambulance and police cars speed down the street. Then maybe ten minutes later, a couple of police officers came over here and told everyone to stay put."

"They told you that Robert Ronaldo had been murdered?" I asked, my voice rising in pitch. "I would have thought they'd notify the next of kin first. That would be Cassie ..."

My voice trailed off as I noticed how pale Scooter had become at the mention of a murder. I pulled the remaining Hershey Kisses out of my purse. "I think this counts as a real emergency," I said as I offered them to him.

As he unwrapped the chocolates and popped them into his mouth, Penny clarified. "I don't know if they've told Cassie Newton about her husband. Ben overheard two of the police officers talking about how Robert Ronaldo had been fatally shot. He came over and told me. Then I told him about the conversation I had overheard about Miguel maybe having a gun."

"But when you heard about the shooting, why did your mind jump to Miguel?" I asked. "He's been here at the party all night. He couldn't have been responsible for the shooting."

Penny shook her head. "His parents were looking for him earlier, but no one has seen him for the past couple of hours. He was so angry about Robert Ronaldo terminating his sister's lease. And if that wasn't enough, remember how Miguel sped off after him the other day? Well, turns out someone saw him deliberately run Robert Ronaldo's car off the road."

She stared at the table and said softly, "I'm ashamed to admit it, but when I heard about what happened, I thought Miguel might be responsible."

"Does anyone else know that Robert Ronaldo has been ... you know ..." I glanced at Scooter. The color had returned to his face. Even so if I mentioned the word "murder" again, I was afraid he would have a relapse.

Fortunately, Penny knew what I meant. "I think the only people who know besides the police are the three of us."

"And Ben," I said.

"I told him not to say anything to anyone, but—"

"Speak of the devil," I muttered as Ben rushed over to us.

He glanced at Scooter and me, before looking at Penny. "Do they know what happened?"

She nodded. "Mollie is the one who found him."

"What does that make now? Five, six ..."

I held up my hand to stop him from tallying up the number of dead bodies I had stumbled upon in Coconut Cove. "Please, now's not the time."

"You're right," the young man said. "It's time for you to get to work."

"Work?" I asked.

"Uh-huh. Once I told Alejandra about how that jerk was killed and that Penny was worried that Miguel was involved, she broke down. I've never seen her like this before." His brow was creased with worry. "Mollie, you have to help."

"Me? How?"

"Clear her brother's name obviously. I already promised Alejandra that you would."

* * *

Early the next morning, I headed to the police station to get an update on the death of Robert Ronaldo. Everyone assumed that he had been murdered, but, during the middle of the night, I realized that there could be another explanation—he had committed suicide with his own gun.

I tried to recall what I had seen by the beach that night. Robert's briefcase was lying in the middle of the path, its contents strewn in the sand. There had been file folders, papers, pens—the usual things you'd expect someone to carry in their briefcase. I sat on a bench outside the station and closed my eyes for a moment, trying to picture what else had been at the scene. The image of a ribbon fluttering in the sea breeze, an envelope with photographs sticking out of it, and a key chain popped into my mind, but not a gun.

I rubbed my eyes. If he had shot himself, wouldn't the gun have been next to his body? Had it been there and I missed seeing it because I was in shock? Maybe the gun had fallen from his hand after he shot himself and when he collapsed, his body landed on top of it.

I took a deep breath. That had to be the answer. It had to have been suicide. That was the simplest explanation and, more importantly, it meant that Miguel would be off the hook.

Despite trying to convince myself of the suicide explanation, the thought of it being murder kept creeping to the forefront of my mind. If it was, given his past, Miguel was likely to be at the top of the list of suspects. Not to mention his desire to stop the new owner of the Seaside Center at all costs from terminating his sister's lease. If that wasn't enough, Miguel had been spotted on Saturday afternoon running Robert Ronaldo's car off the road and threatening him.

As I walked up the steps to the police station, I felt my stomach twist into knots as I recalled how Alejandra and her parents had pleaded with me to clear Miguel's name. Even Scooter, who normally tried to talk me out of getting involved in murder investigations, relented at the sight of tears streaming down both Alejandra and Josefina's cheeks.

"Please let it be suicide," I said to myself as I approached the front desk.

A middle-aged woman with strawberry blonde hair piled into a messy bun on the top of her head, greeted me cheerfully. "How can I help you today, honeybunch?"

"Oh, are you the new receptionist?" I asked.

"Sure am. It's my second day on the job," she said. "Charmaine Buttercup at your service."

"It's nice to meet you, Charmaine …" I hesitated, not sure if 'Buttercup' was part of her first name or if it was her last name.

"You can call me Char," she said, waving her hand in the air. "All my friends do. Not that I have any friends in Coconut Cove. I need some friends here, don't you think?"

When I raised my eyebrows, she laughed. "The look on your face is priceless. I bet you're thinking that the reason I don't have any friends is because I'm a serial killer. Did you see that movie? The one where the lady moves to a new town, tries to make friends with the locals, but they don't want anything to do with her, because her feet smell funny in a real suspicious way. You know on account of the—"

I managed to get a word in edgewise, hazarding a guess. "Bowling shoes?"

"A serial killer who wears bowling shoes? Nope, haven't seen that movie, but that does sound real good." She grinned. "But you don't need to worry about me, honeybunch. In the first place, I don't know how to bowl and, in the second place, if I was a serial killer, I wouldn't be working at the police station, now would I?"

She paused to take a breath, then continued, "Unless, of course, I was a really good serial killer and hadn't been caught yet, then maybe I would be working here. Hmm ... that sounds like a real good plot for a movie. But I'm not an actress." She tucked a stray strand of hair behind her ear. "Although, my husband says that I do have movie star looks. We just moved to Coconut Cove. Did you know that—"

I held up my hand to stop her stream of consciousness. "Sorry to interrupt, Char, it's just that I'm in a bit of a hurry. Do you know if the chief is in?"

"No, honeybunch, he's not. Why don't you give me your name and number, then I'll have him give you a call when he gets back?"

I hesitated. The former receptionist had been well-trained by the chief to throw out any messages I left. Should I give Charmaine Buttercup a fake name so that my message would get through? Maybe something like Louella Daffodil?

I shook my head, realizing that my plan wouldn't work unless I got a burner phone to use. That way the chief wouldn't realize the number belonged to me. While the burner phone idea had merit, it would end up costing me too much in the long run as I'd have to keep tossing and replacing them to stay ahead of the chief.

Charmaine Buttercup looked at me, her pen poised over a notepad. "So, what was your name, honeybunch?"

"Um … Mollie McGhie."

She leaned back in her chair and threw her hands up. "No way! Seriously, you're Mollie McGhie?"

"You've heard of me?"

"Heard of you? I've been dying to

meet you."

I furrowed my brow. "You have?"

"I sure have. I've been a member of FAROUT since forever. Like I was starting to tell you, my hubby and I just moved to Coconut Cove from Arkansas. His name is Dale. We're high school sweethearts. He's a truck driver, you know. Have you ever ridden in a semi-truck?"

"No, I haven't," I said, suppressing a smile. I couldn't even begin to imagine how the chief hired Charmaine. It must have been an impulsive move on his part—there's no way she would have made it through a formal interview. Rambling answers about serial killers and truck drivers, not to mention being a member of FAROUT, would have been too much for him.

She tapped her pen on the desk to get my attention. "Anyhoo, I was a member of the local FAROUT branch back in Arkansas. I love your articles in the monthly magazine." She yanked open her top desk drawer, nearly toppling backward in her chair in the process. "In fact, I think I have a copy in here. Yep, here it is."

"Wow, that's an old one," I said. "I lost all of my back issues in a fire."

"Oh, no, that's a shame." She stood and came around the desk, holding up her phone. "Do you mind if I get a selfie with you?"

"Uh, sure."

After she put her arm around me and snapped a few pictures, she said, "I bet you're a busy lady, but would you mind giving me your autograph? You could sign this here magazine."

As I scrawled my signature next to a picture of a UFO sighting at the Badlands National Park in South Dakota, I asked Charmaine if Chief Dalton knew that she was a FAROUT member.

"No, it didn't come up when I came in

for an interview yesterday. We got to talking about what the best fertilizer is for roses and ..." She snapped her fingers. "... before you know it, an hour had vanished just like that."

"So he actually interviewed you?"

She nodded. "We had a great time. It was more of a social visit, if you know what I mean."

"Probably best not to mention FAROUT to him," I advised, handing the magazine back to her.

She put her hand over her mouth. "Oh … Is he not a believer?"

"Not at all."

"Hmm … well, we'll see about that," she said. "I'm pretty good at convincing people. Just ask my husband. There was this time that I wanted to go target shooting over by the—"

"I'm sorry to interrupt," I said. "But I really do need to see the chief. You wouldn't happen to know where he is, would you?"

"Well, of course, I do, silly. That's my job, isn't it, to keep track of the chief's whereabouts. He's at the Sailor's Corner Cafe. He said he needed some quiet time. Did you know there was a murder last night?"

My shoulders slumped. "So it was murder," I said quietly.

"It sure was, darling. Someone shot that poor fella in the head. And with his own gun too. It was found by the side of the path. Wiped clean of course. No fingerprints on it. Best they can figure is that he kept a loaded gun in his briefcase. For some reason, he opened the briefcase, and the killer got a hold of the gun."

Charmaine paused to catch her breath, then continued speaking so rapidly that I struggled to follow her at times. "Can you believe that happened here? Dale was just about beside himself when I told him what happened. One of the reasons we moved to

Coconut Cove was because it was supposed to be a nice, quiet, safe town. Now Dale is talking about moving again, but I put my foot down. We're going to give it at least a year. It's going to take me at least that long to get my roses blooming again."

She slapped her hand on her thigh. "Wait a minute, were you the lady who found the body?" I nodded. "I heard someone mention the name Mollie, but I never put two and two together."

I started to speak, but she interrupted. "Do you like chocolate?"

"Uh-huh."

"She pulled a candy dish out of her top drawer and set it in front of me. "Go on, help yourself. I know I always need a little pick-me-up when something bad happens. Besides, if you found a dead body, well, I reckon there ain't nothing worse than that."

After I had a couple of pieces of chocolate, Charmaine Buttercup sent me on my way. "You better get going, honeybunch, and catch the chief. I'm sure he'll want to talk to you about the murder."

I smiled at her, grateful for her help and the chocolate. Probably by the next time I saw her Chief Dalton would have set her straight about how little he really wanted to talk with me about murders, UFO sightings, or proposing again to Anabel.

* * *

"Hi, Mollie. Is Scooter parking the car?" Jim, the owner of the Sailor's Corner Cafe, smiled at me as he grabbed a couple of menus from the hostess station.

"No, it's just me today," I said. "New shirt?"

"Like it?" he asked. "Thomas has decided to start designing Hawaiian shirts. This is a prototype."

"It looks great." I peered at the pattern of colorful sailboats, palm trees, and dolphins. "I might have to get one for Scooter."

"I'll let you know when they're for sale," he said. "It's pretty quiet in here this morning, so sit wherever you like and a waitress will be right with you."

I grabbed a menu from Jim and made a beeline to where Chief Dalton was sitting by the window. "Ooh, what do you have there?" I asked as I slid into the booth. "That looks delicious."

The chief scowled. "What do you think it looks like? It's pie."

"I can see that," I said. "But the question is, what kind of pie?" When he didn't answer, I pulled the plate toward me. "Apple. Ooh, good choice. Do you mind handing me that fork?"

"Fork? What do you need a fork for? You haven't ordered anything."

When he didn't budge, I reached across the table and grabbed the unused fork next to his elbow. "Sometimes, they put too much cinnamon in. I want to try it before I order a slice."

"You want to try some of *my* pie?" Before I could answer, his phone rang. He glanced at the screen. "I need to take this."

"Go ahead."

"In private," he said, pressing the phone against his ear.

I waved my hand around the empty cafe. "There's no one here to overhear you."

He scowled, obviously not pleased with what the person on the phone was saying to him, then got up from the table.

"Chief, about the pie—can I try some?"

He glanced at me, nodded, then walked toward the back of the cafe.

After taking a small bite and determining it had the perfect amount of cinnamon, I motioned the waitress over. "Can I get a slice of apple pie, please?"

"Sorry, Mollie. The chief got the last slice. Can I get you a piece of coconut cream?"

I shuddered. There was nothing worse than coconut in my book. Unfortunately, living in a town with coconut in its name meant that local establishments served a lot of dishes with that vile ingredient. Sometimes, they even put coconut in without telling you about it. Have you ever heard of spaghetti made out of coconut? I don't recommend it.

Seeing the expression on my face, the waitress suggested peach pie instead. While I waited for her to return, I eyed up the chief's plate. Surely, he wouldn't mind if I had one more tiny bite? A small piece of apple was sitting on the side of the plate. It looked sad and lonesome all by itself. I scooped it up with my fork and popped it into my mouth. Delicious.

Then I noticed that the pie looked

uneven. Chief Dalton liked things to look neat and tidy. If I cut another piece off the bottom, just so, it would give the slice a nice, clean edge. It sounded like a good plan, but as I positioned my fork above the plate, my hand slipped, slicing the pie into several messy, irregular-shaped pieces. There was no way that the chief was going to believe it was an accident.

"Here you go, Mollie," the waitress said as she set a piece of peach pie in front of me.

As I pulled the plate toward me, I frowned. It looked so ... orange. Completely unappetizing compared to the chief's apple pie. Still it did have one redeeming quality—it was a perfectly shaped piece of pie with no fruit haphazardly sitting on the edge of the plate. The chief had mentioned before how much he enjoys peaches. What if I swapped the two plates?

It sounded like a sensible plan. He'd

eat the piece of pristine peach pie and I'd finish off the rather mangled apple pie. What could go wrong?

"What's this?" The chief asked as he returned to the table.

"Pie," I said slowly.

"This isn't my pie."

"Of course it is. It's on your side of the table."

"The fruit is orange."

"Yeah, too much cinnamon. Gives apples that orange hue."

He took a small mouthful and grimaced. "Nope. Not apple. This is peach."

"That happened to Scooter the other day. He drank hot coffee and burned his taste buds. Everything tasted the same to him. That's probably why your apples taste like peaches."

"I don't like peach pie."

"Good thing you've got a nice slice of apple there then. So who was on the phone?"

"Nice try."

"What do you mean?"

"Stop trying to change the subject."

"Fine. What were we talking about?"

"We weren't talking about anything. You came over here, sat at my table and ate my pie. You're like the Goldilocks of Coconut Cove."

I crumpled up my napkin and said firmly, "Goldilocks complained a lot. I haven't complained about anything."

"Yet," he said dryly.

"Tell you what, why don't we change the subject. How about an Elvis theme? That's a classic."

"An Elvis theme? You're making even less sense than normal," he said before raising his mug to his lips.

"I mean for when you propose to Anabel."

The chief coughed, almost spitting up his coffee.

"See what did I tell you about it being too hot," I said. "Blow on it first or put some more cream in it to cool it down."

He set the mug on the table. "What makes you think I'm going to propose?"

"Well, you love her, right?"

He held my gaze for a moment, then became absorbed in polishing his knife with a napkin.

"Okay, I get it," I said. "You're a tough guy. It's hard for you to talk about mushy stuff. Let's just take it as a given that you're in love with her. The two of you are spending a lot of time together lately. It's obvious you regret divorcing her."

He looked at me sharply. "Why do you think I was the one who divorced her?"

"You're right. It makes more sense that she left you."

"That's not what I meant," he spluttered.

"Anyway, the past is the past. We're here to talk about the future … and the murder, of course."

He folded his arms across his chest.

"I'm not discussing the murder with you."

I shrugged. "Fine, let's talk about the proposal instead. So here's what I was thinking. The first time you got married was in Graceland and the two of you love Elvis. So how about if you dress up like him and sing her one of his romantic ballads—I'll let you decide which one would be best. Then we can tie the engagement ring around Frick or Frack's neck. He could walk toward her while you're on bended knee. Then you could take the ring off and present it to her. That would be a really cute touch."

He took a bite of his peach pie, then quietly asked, "Engagement ring?"

"Good point," I said. "Are you going to buy her a new one or use the one you gave her last time?"

"I never said I was proposing to her," he mumbled.

I watched as he ate another bite of pie, then said, "I think you should use the old one. It's sentimental. And obviously Anabel loves it since she's been wearing it on her right hand for the past couple of months. The trick will be getting it away from her. Do you think she wears it all the time? Does she take it off before she showers or before she goes to bed? I can sneak in and steal it."

He pushed back his now empty pie plate and looked at me indignantly. "Steal it? You want to commit a crime?"

"Well, it's not really a crime if I'm doing it for the chief of police, is it?"

He held up his hands. "You know what, and I can't believe I'm saying this, I'd much rather talk with you about the murder than about this ridiculous proposal scenario you've concocted."

"Super," I said, digging into my purse and pulling out my notebook. "Now what should we start with—the list of suspects or the murder weapon."

"Surely with your deductive powers

you can figure out that the victim was killed with a gun."

"I'm not sure I like this side of you," I said. "I don't think sarcasm suits you at all. Of course, I know it was a gun. But what happened to it? I didn't see it at the crime scene."

"I'm surprised you didn't take a picture."

I shook my head. "I'm upset about that too. I had left my phone in the car— that's why Scooter and I were walking to the parking lot."

"I'm already aware of that, Mrs. McGhie." He tapped his fingers on the table. "Remember, I'm the one that took your statement."

"Tell you what, let's change tacks." I leaned forward. "By the way, did you know that's a sailing term? Tacking means you keep turning the bow of your boat in the wind. It's kind of like zig-zagging along the water. Until we got *Marjorie Jane*, I used to always think that meant you were changing tacks, like those things you put on bulletin boards."

"Your conversational style is zig-zaggy," the chief noted.

"Fine, let's talk suspects. And before you say anything, it's not Miguel Lopez. Alejandra and his parents swear he wouldn't kill anyone."

"Yes, because family are usually such good character witnesses."

I put my pen down. "I agree. They wouldn't want to think the worst about him. And yes, he got into some trouble in high school, but I can't believe he'd actually murder someone. No, it has to be one of the tenants at the shopping center. They were furious that he was trying to terminate their leases."

"Alejandra Lopez is a tenant."

"It wasn't Alejandra either, and you know it." When the chief didn't respond, I added, "Or it could have been Robert Ronaldo's wife. She was having an affair. I bet you didn't know that," I said triumphantly.

He cocked his head to one side. "An affair?"

"Oh, sure, now you want to hear what I have to say. But this is a two-way street. You tell me something in exchange, then I'll tell you about the affair."

"Fine. Mr. Ronaldo was killed with his own gun."

"Not so fast. I knew that already."

"You did?"

I backtracked, not wanting to get my new friend, Charmaine Buttercup, in trouble. "I mean, I surmised that. Was there any sign of a struggle? How did the killer get his gun?"

"I don't have time for this. Tell me about Mr. Ronaldo's wife."

I shrugged. "I saw her with a much younger man on Saturday morning."

"How do you know they were having an affair?"

"I don't think you passionately kiss someone like the two of them were kissing unless you're more than friends."

"What's his name?"

I shook my head. "Two-way street, remember?"

"Fine. The preliminary coroner's report indicates that there wasn't a struggle."

"Interesting," I said as I jotted this new bit of information down in my notebook. "Then the killer and Robert Ronaldo must have known each other."

He shrugged. "Your turn. What's the man's name?"

"No idea."

The chief scowled. "You said that this was a two-way street and that you would tell me the man's name once I gave you a piece of information."

"No, you asked me what his name was. I never said that I knew it. If you had asked me a question that I knew the answer to, I would have given you that piece of information."

"Call me if you have any useful information to share," he said as he got up from the table.

I took a sip of coffee and watched as he walked to the cashier station. Then he abruptly turned back to me and asked quietly, "Do you really think she wouldn't want a new ring?" Before I could answer, he spun on his heels. "Never mind. Forget I said that."

I drank the rest of my coffee while I thought about what the chief and I had discussed. Had Robert Ronaldo known his killer? Who didn't have an alibi for the time that he had been killed?

While I pondered this, the waitress handed me my check.

"Hang on," I said. "There's charges for two pieces of pie on here."

"The chief said that you wouldn't mind paying for both since you ate his apple pie."

* * *

Later that afternoon, I took Mrs. Moto and the Dalton's Yorkies to the waterfront park. Anabel had custody of Frick and Frack on Tuesdays. Since she had an exhibition of her paintings at an art gallery in Miami and wouldn't be back until the next day, she had asked me if I'd take them out for a walk and then drop them off with the chief for the night.

I had readily agreed—Mrs. Moto loved spending time with her canine friends and I was hoping that they could role model proper behavior when walking on a leash. My calico had a tendency to slip out of her harness unnoticed, leaving me on more than one occasion dragging a leash without a cat attached for quite a while before realizing it.

However, instead of teaching the calico proper leash etiquette, the three of them got their leads tangled up chasing after a squirrel. As I bent down to untangle them, my phone rang. I reached into my purse to get it, lost my balance and fell onto the ground.

"Did I catch you at a bad time?" Anabel asked.

"I'm fine," I said inspecting my scraped knee before looking at the three animals, all of whom had adopted poses of angelic innocence. "We've had a little squirrel incident." The two Yorkies climbed onto my lap and yapped. "I think they hear their mom."

I held the phone up to them. After a few moments of barking—on the dogs' part, not Anabel's—I pressed it back to my ear.

"I have some interesting information for you. Cassie Newton was at the art gallery today. She had been in town to see her lawyer and came in afterward."

"Her lawyer? Do you know why? Was it about her husband's estate?"

"No idea," Anabel said. "But it does raise a good point—is she the new owner of the Seaside Center?"

"That's a good question. If she is, will she still terminate their leases? I'll see if Scooter can find anything out about it." The Yorkies and Mrs. Moto rolled over on their backs and I scratched their bellies, then continued, "Don't you think it's odd that she's hanging out at an art gallery? Not exactly what you normally do when you're in mourning."

"That's what I thought. Turns out she had commissioned some pop art paintings of her favorite tennis shoes from an artist friend of mine for a place she just bought in Florida. She came in to check on them."

"She has a place in Florida?" I asked.

"Yeah, a condo in one of those ritzy buildings in Miami Beach. After she left, I asked my friend about it. He said that when she first came in a month ago, she told him that her husband would hate the paintings. When my friend asked her why she was going to hang up paintings that he wouldn't like, she told him that her husband would be long gone by the time they were completed."

"Long gone? Wow, does that mean what I think it means?"

"I don't know," she said. "My friend assumed Cassie meant that she was getting a divorce but now ..."

"Now that her husband has been murdered, it could have meant something else entirely," I said slowly.

"Exactly," Anabel said. "Anyway, I told Tiny about it, but I thought I'd tell you as well as you're looking into things for the Lopez family."

"Thanks, I appreciate that," I said. "Can we catch up tomorrow when you get back to Coconut Cove?"

"Yeah, that would be great. There was something else that happened when I spoke with Tiny. It was kind of strange." Anabel hesitated for a moment, then continued. "He asked me if I wear the engagement ring that he gave me all the time or if I take if off at night. Don't you think that's odd?"

"That's very interesting," I said. "The peach pie seems to have done the trick."

"Peach pie? What does pie have to do with anything? Oh, wait a minute, a customer just came in. You can tell me more about the pie tomorrow."

After she hung up, I bent down to check on my furry companions. "I think your daddy is going to propose to your mommy," I whispered to the Yorkies as I straightened out their leashes again.

As they ran around in circles, tangling themselves back up in the process, I noticed that Kyle was sitting on a nearby bench speaking on his phone. I inched over in his direction, taking care not to trip over Mrs. Moto, who was sunning herself on the sidewalk, conspicuously leash and harness-free.

"I'm telling you. I showed him the proof. But then he refused to pay me," I overheard Kyle saying as I neared where he was seated. After a beat, he added, "I don't know what to do."

He reached into his suit jacket pocket pulling out a red-and-white striped envelope that looked just like the one Cassie Newton had given him at the Tipsy Pirate. As he opened the flap, I could see a wad of money crammed inside. He yanked the bills out and started thumbing through them, then seemed to realize that counting large sums of cash in public probably wasn't the brightest idea.

Kyle stuffed the money back into the envelope, rose from the bench and starting walking toward the public dock. The last thing I heard him say before he was out of earshot was, "You think I should keep the cash?"

I sat on the bench he had just vacated, Frick and Frack on either side of me, and shook my head. There were too many mysteries to wrap my head around. Not only had Robert Ronaldo been killed, but Alejandra's ex-boyfriend was walking around with money that Cassie Newton had given him. Also, it wasn't American money either. The bills were colorful, not that boring green you find on notes printed by the US Treasury.

"Any ideas, boys?" I asked the Yorkies. "Your daddy is a police officer. You must have learned a thing or two listening to him. Where do you think the money is from? Why did Cassie give it to him? And what proof does Kyle have and who wouldn't pay him for it?"

The only response I got from Frick and Frack were yawns. Taking their cue from Mrs. Moto, they snuggled down, their heads on my lap, and settled in for an afternoon nap.

CHAPTER 6
FUNNY MONEY

After Frick and Frack woke up from their naps, and I found Mrs. Moto's harness and leash hidden behind a palm tree, the four of us headed to the police station so that I could drop the dogs off with Chief Dalton. As I walked into the lobby, the Yorkies tugged on their leashes. They knew that this was where their daddy worked, and they were eager to be reunited with him. After I unclipped them, they bounded over to Charmaine Buttercup.

"Well, who do we have here?" she

asked as they vied for her attention. While she petted them, Mrs. Moto jumped onto Charmaine's desk and proceeded to knock her desk organizer over.

After gently scolding Mrs. Moto and apologizing to Charmaine, I quickly scooped up some paper clips before they joined the pens on the floor.

"No problem, honeybunch. I have two cats myself. One's a calico much like yours. His name is Bobby Joe. But he isn't a bobtail. My other cat is named Darlene Sue. She's a Persian. Sheds hair everywhere, which drives Dale nuts —"

Charmaine paused to move a ceramic figurine out of Mrs. Moto's way, then opened up one of her desk drawers. "I think I might have something in here for you. Do you like tuna flavor?" she asked, pulling a container of cat treats out.

Mrs. Moto meowed, then nudged

Charmaine's hand insistently.

"I think that's her way of saying yes," I said with a smile.

As she fed the calico a treat, the Yorkies yapped and tried to climb up her legs.

"Do you think they'd eat these?" Charmaine inspected the container. "I got it from the pet store for my cats, but it doesn't say anything about whether you can feed them to dogs."

"The chief has a bag of peanut butter and bacon dog biscuits for them in his office," I said. "Where is he, by the way? You'd think he would have heard these two barking even from back there and come out by now."

"Cassie Newton phoned and asked him to come see her," Charmaine said.

"Where at? Her boat? I haven't seen her at the marina since her husband was killed."

"No, she's staying at the Hazelton Estate."

"That's odd," I said. "I thought the estate had been closed up while the owner is ... um ... away."

"Apparently, there's a caretaker on the property." Charmaine scooped the Yorkies up and set them on her lap while Mrs. Moto sprawled on her keyboard. "The chief said that the owner, Everett Hazelton, is gone for a while so he has someone keeping an eye on things."

"I'm pretty sure Everett isn't enjoying his current accommodations nearly as much as he did the estate." I shuddered as I recalled the events that had led to the unpleasant man's change of residence. "But how did Cassie Newton end up at the estate? I didn't realize that she knew anyone in Coconut Cove."

"Apparently, the caretaker is a friend of hers." Charmaine frowned as she stroked the Yorkies. "Before I transferred her call to the chief, she told me that she couldn't bear to stay on her boat, because it reminded her too much of her husband. I can't imagine how I'd cope if I lost my Dale."

It seemed odd that *Factoid* reminded Cassie of her husband. She hadn't seemed to be thinking about him when I saw her in a passionate embrace with another man.

"Do you know why she wanted to see the chief?" I asked.

Charmaine took the lid off her candy dish and offered me a dark chocolate mint. Then she lowered her voice. "She said that she knew who killed her husband."

"Did she tell you who?" I swallowed hard, hoping the answer wasn't Miguel.

She shook her head. "No, the chief got off the other line and I put the call through."

"Did he say when he'd be back?"

"No, he rushed out before I could ask him."

"I'm not sure what to do with these

two." I pointed at the dogs squirming on her lap. As much as I loved Frick and Frack, they could be a little too energetic at times. What I needed now was some peace and quiet to figure out what to do next. "He's supposed to take care of them while his ex-wife is out of town."

"That's easy, honeybunch. Leave them with me."

"Are you sure? Won't they get in the way?"

"Not at all. They'll be good company while I work." She patted a stack of file folders on the corner of her desk. "You wouldn't believe how disorganized everything is. I found these on top of the microwave in the break room. Everyone was too scared to go in there on account of the mud daubers."

"Well, if you're sure." While I handed Charmaine the Yorkie's leashes, Mrs. Moto snaked her paw around the computer monitor and pushed the folders onto the floor.

I shook my head at the cat. "This is how you repay the nice lady after she gave you a treat?" As I replaced the folders back on the desk, I noticed one of them had a familiar name written on it —Kyle Kaminski, the guy who had swept Alejandra off her feet, then broke her heart. The same guy who I had seen earlier holding a wad of foreign money in his hand.

Before I could ask Charmaine why there was a police file on Kyle, her phone rang. While she explained how to contest a speeding ticket, I sat in a chair, trying to use my telepathic powers to will Mrs. Moto into knocking the folders off the desk again so that I could get a closer look at Kyle's file. Instead, she jumped on top of them and curled up into a ball.

Just like a cat—the minute you want them to knock stuff on the floor, they decide a nap is called for.

* * *

After twenty minutes, Charmaine was still listening to the caller complain about the speed trap in Coconut Cove, and Mrs. Moto was still napping atop the file folders. I finally gave up on both of them, waved goodbye to Charmaine and carried the sleeping calico out of the police station.

Main Street was teeming with people —tourists window shopping, locals getting off work, and folks meeting friends for drinks or an early dinner. I decided to slip into the newly opened rose garden which had been established in a courtyard off of one of side streets. It was a peaceful place, away from the buzz of Coconut Cove's downtown.

As I sat on one of the benches—Mrs. Moto snuggled up beside me—I tried to figure out my next steps in the investigation of Robert Ronaldo's murder. My biggest concern was not knowing who Cassie Newton was going to name as her husband's murderer. What if she said that it was Miguel? Would Chief Dalton arrest him right away? How would Alejandra and her parents cope?

The logical side of my brain was one hundred percent certain that Miguel's name wouldn't come up in conversation between the chief and Cassie. After all, Miguel was innocent. Alejandra and her parents believed that, and so did I. There had to be someone else that she was going to finger as the killer.

Except ... my gut was telling me something different. It was one hundred percent certain that Cassie was going to blame Miguel. Unfortunately, my gut was usually right. If Miguel wasn't already at the top of the chief's list of suspects, he would be after Cassie was done speaking with him. I needed to figure out who really killed Robert Ronaldo, and fast.

After popping some M&M'S in my mouth for an energy boost, I opened up my notebook. Thankfully, Mrs. Moto was still asleep and not trying to distract me from my investigation by batting my limited edition glitter pen out of my hand. For some reason, she seemed fascinated by its unicorn design, taking every opportunity she could to run off with it, and stashing it in one of her many hiding spots aboard our boat.

I flipped through the pages until I got to the two groups of suspects I had jotted down earlier—people from Coconut Cove and outsiders. Briefly distracted by Mrs. Moto's legs twitching while she slept, I wondered what she was dreaming about. Probably chasing seagulls on the beach. She loved living in Coconut Cove as much as Scooter and me. While I stroked one of her paws, I wondered how long we would need to live here before we would be considered locals.

As I tapped my pen on the page, I frowned. That's what made this so difficult—one of the people under the "Coconut Cove Locals" heading could be a murderer. The list of names was pretty straightforward. It consisted solely of the tenants of the Seaside Center. They were all disgruntled with Robert Ronaldo, because he had terminated their leases. Even so had one of them been angry enough to have killed him, because of it?

I had seen Angus Tanaka shove Robert Ronaldo the night of Alejandra's grand opening party, and I had heard the owner of the bookstore speak in pretty strong terms about what he'd like to do to make the new landlord see reason. As for the other tenants, I wasn't sure how angry and upset they were— would they have gone as far as murder?

Rubbing my eyes, I tallied up how many interviews I would need to have. Maybe four or five since there was

Angus Tanaka, the man who ran the deli, the florist, the couple who owned the pet store, and the proprietor of the bookstore.

Then it hit me—I might not need to interview all of them if I could establish who had the opportunity to kill Robert Ronaldo. Did any of the tenants have an alibi? Who among them was unaccounted for when he was killed? I shook my head at the rookie investigator mistake I had made—alibis first, then interviews. Maybe the chief was right and I didn't deserve my FAROUT investigative reporter badge.

I sighed, then flipped the page over in my notebook. Making a note on my To Do List to look into the tenants' alibis, I looked at the only name that I had under the "Outsider" label—Cassie Newton.

She had been having an affair, obviously unhappily married. Had she wanted out from her marriage? She had seemed to imply as much to Anabel's artist friend, telling him that her husband wouldn't be an issue when it came to what paintings she hung in her new condo. Was that because she planned on divorcing her husband ... or, worse, killing him? If she had been intent on getting rid of him in a more permanent way, where did her boyfriend fit in? Had he been involved in the murder? Maybe even without Cassie's knowledge?

I scribbled 'look into boyfriend' under Cassie's name, but before I could jot down any further notes, my pen went flying out of my hand.

"Done with your nap?" I asked Mrs. Moto as she leaned over the bench and peered at the pen lying on the ground.

She looked up at me and meowed plaintively.

"No, I'm not going to pick it up right now. I can brainstorm my ideas out loud rather than jot them down." I scooped the calico up and held her against my chest. "What do you think? Could there be some other outsider who came to Coconut Cove to murder Robert Ronaldo? I should look into his background."

Mrs. Moto squirmed out of my arms, then darted over to a wooden sign at the entrance to the garden entrance. She stretched up on her hind legs, pressed her front paws against the signpost, and yowled.

"Are you ready to go?" I bent down to pick her up, but she dashed away. After tearing across the courtyard and running around the rose bushes that Mrs. McDougal had donated, she ran back toward the sign. I tried to catch her as she frantically circled the sign post. Finally managing to snag her, I grasped her firmly in my arms.

I pointed at the sign. "Since you can't read, I'll tell you what this says. 'Park Rules: Number one—skateboards and bicycles are prohibited. Number two— clean up after your pets.'" Mrs. Moto meowed sharply. "Yes, I know that one doesn't apply to you, because you're smarter than dogs and know how to use a litter box."

Mrs. Moto purred in agreement, then pressed her paw over rule number three. Gently moving her aside, I continued. "'No alcohol to be consumed on the premises.' That one's fine with me. Now, if they banned chocolate, then I'd have to start a protest. The last rule is the one that applies to you—'all pets need to be on leashes.'"

Mrs. Moto stopped purring and started meowing insistently

"I know you don't like wearing it, but—"

Twisting in my arms, she pressed her paw on the sign again and yowled.

"I think someone needs another nap. This sign is getting you too excited," I said. "How about if I take you back to the boat before I go to the nail salon to check on Alejandra?"

* * *

When I pushed the door of the nail salon open, there was a buzz in the air. Two women sat in the spa chairs, sipping on coffee and gossiping while Francine and another nail technician gave them pedicures. Two teenaged girls were sitting in the reception area, giggling as they took selfies with their new manicures.

Alejandra was at one of the manicure stations working on another teenager's nails. She waved me over. "Look how cute these are," she said, pointing at the designs she had applied—pom-poms, footballs, and megaphones. "All the cheerleaders are getting their nails done before the Homecoming game."

"They're cute, but I think I prefer mine," I said.

The bubbly teenager leaned over and squealed as she admired my nails. "Ooh, I want to get something like that next time. I love the baby Yoda on your ring finger."

I perched in a chair next to Alejandra and watched as she finished up the cheerleader's nails. I was in awe of her artistic talent, especially her ability to make things look so realistic on such a relatively small amount of space.

"I have a few minutes before my next appointment," Alejandra said after the girls left. "Why don't we have some coffee?"

While she popped into the back to get our drinks, I overheard Francine talking to her client.

"Between you and me, it's a good thing Alejandra hired me," she said while she massaged the woman's feet. "She doesn't know the first thing about running a nail salon. These young girls with their trendy ideas. I don't think she's going to last very long, do you?"

The woman gave a non-committal answer while Francine applied lotion to her calves. Undeterred, she continued, "I used to own a nail salon in St. Louis. It was very successful." She looked around the salon, her silver corkscrew curls bouncing around her head. "If I owned this place, I'd make some changes, like—"

Francine abruptly stopped speaking when she saw Alejandra emerge from the back carrying two steaming mugs. Alejandra smiled brightly at the women getting pedicures, then turned to me and suggested that we sit up front.

Once we were settled in the comfortable chairs in the reception area, Alejandra's smile faded. "Is there any news on the investigation?" she asked quietly.

I chewed on my lip for a moment, debating whether to tell her that Cassie Newton was in the process of telling the chief who she thought killed her husband. I decided against it—no reason to get Alejandra worried until I knew exactly what it was that Cassie had said. The dark circles under my young friend's eyes worried me. Even her carefully applied make-up couldn't hide her lack of sleep. Concern over her brother, what had happened with Kyle, and the future of her nail salon was clearly eating her up.

"Nothing to report," I said. "But I'm working on it. What I was wondering was if you knew if anyone had an alibi for the time when Robert Ronaldo was killed?"

She sipped on her coffee and stared out the window. "Hmm … let's see. The party was winding down and most people had left by then, except for my fellow tenants and my parents. My mother brought out some champagne for a toast. She poured, and I handed out the glasses."

"Was there anyone missing?"

"Now that you mention it, Angus wasn't there." She looked down at the floor. "And neither was Miguel."

"Where was Miguel?" I asked.

"All he'll say is that he went for a walk to clear his head." As she set her mug on the table, I noticed that her hand was shaking. She took a deep breath, then looked at me, her brow creased with worry. "My mom called when I was in the back. Chief Dalton wants to see Miguel at the police station later today. What is he going to do? He doesn't have an alibi."

"Don't worry about it. I'm sure it's just routine. The police will be talking to everyone."

"You're probably right." She folded her hands in her lap and stared at them, lost in thought. She looked up sharply as the door to the salon swung open. When she saw the young guy standing there, looking around the salon uncertainly, Alejandra straightened her shoulders and smiled warmly. "Can I help you?"

He grinned back at her. "Yes, I'd like

to make an appointment for a manicure."

While Alejandra booked a time for him to come in later that evening, I carried the mugs to the back. As I neared the kitchen area, I almost collided with Francine, causing her to drop a pile of towels.

"Sorry about that," I said as I helped her pick them up. I pointed at the front of the nail salon. "Looks like things are getting busy in here. That guy just booked an appointment."

"We've been getting a lot of business," Francine said. "Between you and me, sweetie, I don't think it will last though. Right now, it's just friends and family trying to support her."

I pointed at the young man chatting with Alejandra. "I don't think he's friends or family. I think this is the first time they met." I cocked my head to one side, curious about how he had ended up at the Nail Nook. "Is it normal for guys to get their nails done?"

"Actually, it's becoming more commonplace these days," Francine said. As she set the towels down on one of the manicure stations, she said, "Back when I first opened my salon, I had one regular male customer. He came in every week, saying that it was important to have nice looking nails. The funny part of it was that he used to be a boxer. You wouldn't think boxers would care about how their hands looked." Her eyes turned flinty. "He was a real—"

Before Francine could finish her train of thought, her client asked to be brought a magazine.

She nodded at the woman, then turned to me. "Gotta go. Let me know if you ever want to try something different on your nails. Maybe a nice ladylike pink, rather than that awful green."

Ignoring her jibe about my nails, I placed the mugs in the sink, then returned to the reception area. "Before I go," I said to Alejandra while I slung my purse over my shoulder. "There's one other thing I wanted to ask you about."

"What's that?" she said, briefly looking up from the computer.

"It's about Kyle."

She took a deep breath. "I definitely don't like the sound of that."

"I saw him earlier this afternoon."

"You did? Where?" she asked, a hopeful tone in her voice.

"He was at the waterfront park. I overheard him talking on his phone."

She smirked. "Overheard or eavesdropped?"

"That's not really important," I said. "What is important is that he was having a really odd phone conversation. He told the other person that he showed someone proof, but they refused to pay him. Do you know what he was talking about?"

"Proof? That is odd." She pondered this for a moment. "Nope, no idea what that was about."

"Do you know who could have owed him money?"

She scratched her head. "Maybe one of his clients?"

"What exactly does he do?"

"He's in business development."

"What does that mean?"

She furrowed her brow. "You know, I'm not exactly sure. We didn't really talk about his business. All I know is that he traveled a lot for it. He was in Coconut Cove doing some sort of deal."

"Was it an international deal?"

"I don't know. Maybe."

"He had an envelope full of cash, but they weren't American bills. They looked foreign."

"Foreign?"

I shrugged. "I'm not sure. But that wasn't the only interesting thing. The envelope the money was in looked exactly like the one that Cassie Newton gave him at the Tipsy Pirate the night of the semi-finals."

"Why would she have given him money?"

"I have no idea. But it's on my list of things to look into. I actually have a lot of questions for her."

Alejandra ran her fingers through her hair, mussing up her French braid. "Sorry, I know I'm asking a lot of you. It's just with Miguel's history, I'm worried that someone will try to pin the murder on him. And Kyle, it's just …"

I squeezed her hand. "It's okay. You focus on your business and leave the rest to me. I'm sure there's a perfectly reasonable explanation for what's going on with Kyle."

CHAPTER 7
DOUBLE THE CHOCOLATE,
HOLD THE FLOWERS

After leaving the nail salon, I went next door to the Himalayan Highlands chocolate shop. Angus was tying one of his trademark tartan bows around a white candy box.

"Here you go," he said, handing it to a man who was rocking back and forth on the balls of his feet. "I think your wife will really enjoy this assortment. She might even forgive you."

The man looked sheepishly at me out

of the corner of his eye, then rushed out of the shop.

"That was a large box," I said. "He must be in some serious trouble."

"Oh, he is." Angus peered out the window and grinned. "Now he's going into the florist. I bet you he walks out with a dozen roses."

"Chocolate and flowers—it's not a bad start to getting your wife to forgive you." I smiled. "Although if it was me, I'd rather have double the chocolate and hold the flowers."

Angus pulled a small box off one of the metal shelves running along the back wall. "Did you want your usual?"

I nodded, and he carefully placed four truffles inside the box, nestling each one in a silver candy cup. Just the thought of the dusting of cocoa powder and the dark ganache center made my mouth water. As he started to cut off a piece of ribbon to adorn the box, I stopped him. "No need for that. I'll probably eat these right away. Having to untie that will just slow me down."

"Too late." He held up the green, blue, red, and white plaid ribbon. "Why don't you take it home for Mrs. Moto to play with?"

"Better yet, I'll tie it around her neck. She lost another one of her collars yesterday, so she needs some sort of adornment."

Angus laughed as he handed me the ribbon. "By 'lost,' you mean she wriggled out of it?"

"Yep. That makes three already this month. I'm going to have to see if I can start buying them in bulk from the pet store." I toyed with the ribbon, trying to picture how it would look against Mrs. Moto's orange and black markings. "What tartan did you say this was again?"

"It belongs to the Mackenzie clan, from my mother's side of the family. I got my red hair from her." He motioned at the lid of my box of truffles. "Take a look at this. I just had a new logo designed. You and the gentleman who just left are the first ones to see it."

"It's cute," I said, torn between admiring the logo and shoving the lid aside and snatching one of the truffles out.

Angus took that decision away from me by pulling the box toward him and pointing out the features of his new logo. "The tartan frame represents my mother. And the *maneki-neko* in the center represents my father's Japanese roots. It means 'beckoning cat' in English. See how it's holding up its paw and waving? *Maneki-neko* are a good luck symbol."

"Just like Mrs. Moto," I said. "A calico Japanese bobtail. Ever since we adopted her, she's brought us good luck. Well, that is except for all the dead bodies I keep stumbling across."

"How many does that make now since

you've moved to Coconut Cove?"

I glanced around the shop uneasily, then mumbled, "Eight."

Angus raised his eyebrows. "Wow, that is a lot."

Feeling my face grow warm, I opened the box and pulled out one of the truffles. I took a bite, then looked up at Angus, saying in a low voice, "It's not like I seek them out."

"Maybe it's good luck that you find them."

"Huh?"

"You've played a big role in solving the murder cases, right?"

I took another bite of my truffle. "I suppose."

"So, that's where your good luck comes into play. If it wasn't for you, killers might be running around on the loose. Coconut Cove is fortunate to have you."

As I finished off the truffle, I thought about what Angus said. If he had killed

Robert Ronaldo, would he be praising my investigative skills? Or was that just a distraction so that I wouldn't think he was guilty?

As I was trying to figure out how to ask delicately about where he was the night of the murder, Angus casually said, "You know, I don't have an alibi for the night of the murder."

"Where were you?" I said, trying to match his casual tone.

He pointed to the rear of the shop. "Back there, working on the books. With my lease being terminated, I needed to figure out my financial position. I had just placed a large order of supplies which was going to impact my cash flow."

"No one saw you working back there?"

He shook his head. "I guess I should have stayed for the champagne toast instead."

"What did the police say?"

"Nothing. They just took notes and

said that they'd follow up with me later."
He shrugged. "I'm innocent, so I don't
have anything to worry about, right?"

I wanted to ask him more questions
about his altercation with the murder
victim during Alejandra's grand opening
party, but before I could, the man who
was in trouble with his wife came back
in the shop bearing a bouquet of roses.

"Angus, I better get another box of
chocolates, just in case."

I left the shop wondering about two
things—what had that man done that
would require two boxes of chocolate
and flowers, and was Angus telling the
truth.

* * *

The next morning, Scooter walked into
the main cabin of our boat and held up
his ukulele. "She broke another string."

Mrs. Moto, who was curled up in my
lap trying her best to look innocent,

gave an indignant meow.

"Yeah, but she was doing a great rendition of *Can't Help Falling in Love* before it happened. It takes talent to play Elvis tunes on a ukulele." I stroked her paws. "I think she needs to get her nails clipped."

Scooter recoiled in horror. "No way am I doing that again. I ended up with scratches everywhere and she ends up with the same long, sharp claws that she started out with."

"Why don't we take her to the pet store and let the professionals take care of it. Then, if she behaves," I looked pointedly at the calico. She blinked slowly at me in return. "If she behaves, we get her some more Purrtastic catnip as a reward."

"Well, I suppose we could try it," Scooter said. "She does need a new collar in any case. Where did you get that ribbon around her neck, anyway?"

"Angus gave it to me yesterday when I

was at the chocolate shop. He ties them around the candy boxes. It's his trademark. Whenever you see one of those ribbons around town, you know that someone has just eaten some of his delicious chocolate. And you should see the new logo he had printed on the boxes—the cat on it looks just like Mrs. Moto."

Scooter smiled. "I doubt I'll ever get a chance to see one of the boxes or the ribbons, considering that anytime you buy something at his shop, you eat it all up before you even get into the car."

I started to protest, but he silenced me with a kiss. "After ten years of marriage, I know you too well, my little chipmunk."

"Are you saying I look like a rodent?"

"Okay, so not a chipmunk. How about my little tortoise?"

"Nah, tortoises have weird eyes."

"Weird? How?"

"They're really tiny and dark. Whenever a tortoise stares at me, I feel uneasy, like it's trying to hypnotize me."

Scooter chuckled. "Do you have many staring contests with tortoises?"

"It happens," I said. "Did you know that they have a third eyelid? Tell me that's not creepy."

"A third eyelid?" Scooter grabbed his tablet off the table. "Ooh. That's a really good piece of trivia. I need to make a note of it. Who knows, that question might come up in the trivia finals."

While I took a sip of coffee, Mrs. Moto readjusted herself on my lap, stretching her front legs out and pressing her paws on Scooter's tablet.

"Hey, I'm working on something important here," he said to her.

"I'm not sure Mrs. Moto would agree that winning the finals is more important than paying attention to her."

Scooter smiled and scratched the top of her head. "You know, she's had this ribbon on since yesterday. Maybe we should just stick with a ribbon instead of shelling out for another collar."

"It's an idea, except there's no way to easily attach a tag with her name and our number to it."

"I'm not sure she needs a tag. Everyone in Coconut Cove knows her and who she belongs to."

"You mean which humans belong to her."

"I stand corrected." Scooter got to his feet and picked the cat up. "Okay. Let's go get those nails trimmed."

As we pulled into the Seaside Center, I rehashed the night of Robert Ronaldo's murder in my head. Of all the tenants, Angus was the only one who didn't have an alibi. The fact that he wasn't concerned about it baffled me though. Even if I knew I was innocent of a crime, I'd still feel anxious knowing that I didn't have any way to prove to the police that I didn't do it.

The only other person who didn't have an alibi for that night was Miguel.

Alejandra had sent me a text the previous night to say that she still didn't know where he had been when they were doing the champagne toast. Concerned that Cassie Newton had named Miguel as her husband's killer, I had texted back to ask if the police had paid another visit to her brother. When she said that they hadn't, I breathed a sigh of relief. Maybe he was in the clear, after all.

My list of suspects was woefully short. There were only three people on it— Angus, Cassie, and Cassie's boyfriend. As I climbed out of the car, my eyes were drawn to the Nail Nook. Robert Ronaldo had been standing outside the nail salon right before his murder, surrounded by the tenants of the shopping plaza. Although one other person had been there—the executive producer of *Triviamania*, Brittany Abernethy. She had barged her way in through the crowd, said something to give Angus and Miguel pause. Then, she had led Robert Ronaldo away.

But where had she led him to? Had it been along the path along the beach? Did they have an argument? Did she grab his gun and shoot him?

Scooter interrupted my thoughts. "Earth to my little ... my little buttercup?"

"I like the flower idea when it comes to pet names—definitely better than some of the others you've come up with for me—but I already know someone with 'buttercup' in her name."

"Okay, back to the drawing board." He put his arm around my shoulders, and we trailed after Mrs. Moto as she led the way to the pet store, clearly oblivious to the fact that her nails were about to be trimmed.

As we entered the store, the calico leaped up onto one of the glass counters and stared down at the containers of catnip displayed beneath her. She kept jabbing her paw over the one containing her favorite blend as though enough pressure would cause the counter to miraculously open and allow her to dive in and roll around in the fragrant leaves.

When she started to extend her claws, I grabbed her before she could leave scratch marks on the glass. "Do you think you could do something about her nails?" I asked the pet store owner.

"Of course," he said as I handed her to him. "Be back in a jiff."

While we waited, anticipating angry yowling to emanate from the grooming station, followed by the pet store owner crying out for an extra large bandage to staunch the flow of blood from the scratches on his arms, Scooter and I examined the cat trees on display.

I ran my hands across one of the carpeted pedestals. "Too bad we can't fit one of these on our boat."

"Our entire boat is a giant cat tree for her," Scooter said. "Haven't you noticed how she loves perching on top of the rolled-up mainsail?"

"Yes, it's a good vantage point to keep an eye on the seagulls."

"She even tried to climb up the mast the other day." He gestured toward the ceiling, demonstrating her antics. "She had almost gotten to the top by sinking her claws into the running rigging and pulling herself up. When she saw me, somehow she managed to turn herself around and make it safely back down."

I gulped. "But it's, what, sixty feet up to the top of the mast? I'm glad I didn't see that. I know cats aren't afraid of heights, but what if she had fallen?"

"That's why cats have nine lives."

"Do you think she'd like something like this?" I pulled out a wand with ribbons attached to it and swished it around in the air. "Oh, hey, speaking of the boat, what are we doing to do about fixing the anchor light?"

Scooter took a step back to avoid

getting hit by the ribbons. "I spoke with Ben. He's going to come by and help. He'll hoist me up the mast. Hopefully, it's just a bad bulb that needs to be replaced."

"Are you sure you want to do that?" I asked. "It sounds dangerous."

"You're a fine one to talk. You're always getting yourself in dangerous situations. Going up the mast is perfectly safe. It's something sailboat owners do all the time." He nudged me. "Unless you want to go up to the top instead? You weigh a lot less than me. It would be easier on Ben."

"No way. You can count me out." I shook my head emphatically. "Ben's a young, strong guy. He'll manage just fine."

"Here she is," the owner of the pet store announced. He was smiling and appeared unscathed. Mrs. Moto was snuggled comfortably in his arms, purring loudly.

I sighed. "I guess she didn't let you near her claws."

"No, it's all done. She enjoyed her little manicure, didn't you?" he cooed.

"She enjoyed getting her nails clipped?" Scooter scratched his jaw. "How in the world did you manage that?"

"Trade secret," he said.

"Well, I guess we know who will be taking care of clipping her nails from now on," Scooter said.

While he was putting our purchases into a bag—a new collar, some Purrtastic catnip, and the ribbon toy—Francine walked in.

"Sorry to interrupt, but I've only got a few minutes. Do you have any of those argyle sweater vests in extra small? I need them for my chihuahua. My daughter keeps the air conditioning on full blast and the poor little thing is freezing. I'm worried he's going to catch a cold."

"Hang on a minute, and I'll check in the back. I think they came in this morning."

While he looked for the sweater vests, Mrs. Moto padded across the counter to Francine. She sat on her haunches and held up her right front paw.

"She looks just like the *maneki-neko* on Angus' new logos," I said.

Francine peered at her. "No, she doesn't look anything like it. The cat on his logo has its other paw up and there's a bell around its neck."

"Maybe we should put a couple of extra bells on Mrs. Moto's collar," Scooter suggested. "The seagulls might stand a chance that way."

"Muhammad Ali loves to chase seagulls too," Francine said.

"Is that your chihuahua's name?" I asked.

"Uh-huh. He's a real fighter. He definitely punches above his weight."

"Do your grand-kids like Muhammad

Ali?"

"They adore him," Francine beamed. "I can't wait to introduce the new grandbaby to him."

"You must be excited to have another one on the way."

"I sure am," she said. "It's the reason why I moved back to Coconut Cove. I think I can make a new life for myself here."

"A new life?" I asked. "What was wrong with your old one? Does it have something to do with that man you were telling me about yesterday?"

She furrowed her brow. "What man?"

"The boxer you used to give manicures to."

She waved her hand in the air. "That was ages ago. Water under the bridge. No, I was talking about my ex-husband. Men, you know what it's like."

I glanced at Scooter who was showing Mrs. Moto the iguanas and snakes in cages on the far wall. "I guess ..."

Francine followed my gaze. "We can't all be as lucky as you," she said crisply.

I nodded. I was lucky indeed, to have Scooter and our fur baby in my life. He looked so happy, holding our fur baby in his arms and cooing at her. I had a feeling his mood was going to sour when I told him what our next stop was.

* * *

"We're going to see Cassie Newton? Did I hear that right?" Scooter asked, blinking rapidly.

We were sitting in the parking lot at the Seaside Center, and I had just informed Scooter that I wanted to go the Hazelton Estate to track down his celebrity crush. "Yep. She was going to tell Chief Dalton who murdered her husband, and I need to know who she named."

"Why?" Scooter said. "Alejandra told you that the police haven't followed up with Miguel. That means she didn't point the finger at him. He's in the clear. You're off the hook with this investigation."

I shook my head. "I can't let this go until I know with absolute certainty who killed Robert Ronaldo. That's the only way that I'll know that Miguel is safe. I owe it to Alejandra."

"Fair enough. But why don't you just ask the chief what she said to him."

I snorted. "Yeah, right. Like he'd tell me anything. I'd have to wheedle it out of him and I don't have time for that. The easiest approach is to go directly to the source—Cassie Newton. She agreed to see us when I called."

Scooter turned the rearview mirror toward him and sighed. "I can't go there looking like this."

"Looking like what?"

He pointed at his temples. "See that gray there."

"Don't be silly." I ran my fingers

through his hair. "The gray makes you look distinguished."

"It does?"

After I reassured him that he was as handsome as ever, then teased him a bit about having a celebrity crush, we pulled up to the gate in front of the Hazelton Estate.

Scooter leaned out the window and pressed the buzzer on the intercom. While we waited for someone to respond, he asked me if I had found out any more about the caretaker.

"No, the only thing that I know is what Charmaine Buttercup said, that the caretaker is Cassie's friend." I cocked my head to one side. "Do you think Everett knows she's staying at his estate?"

Scooter frowned. "I hope so. He isn't a guy you want to get on the wrong side of. Remember what he did to—"

"How can I help you?" a deep voice boomed over the intercom.

"We're here to see Ca ... Ca ..." Scooter started hyperventilating, unable to say the name of his celebrity crush out loud.

I leaned across him. "We have an appointment with Cassie Newton. I phoned earlier. It's Mollie and Scooter McGhie."

"Proceed up the driveway, ma'am," the man replied as the gates swung open.

When the car didn't move, I tugged Scooter's arm. "You can drive through."

"This is a bad idea." He was gripping the steering wheel so tightly that I feared he might leave permanent indentations in it. "We can't interrogate Ca ... Ca ..."

"Interrogate is a strong word. All we're going to do is have a friendly chat with her. Maybe she'll even give you her autograph."

He released his grip on the steering wheel and looked at me, his eyes shining. "You think so?"

"I'm sure she will."

After parking in the circular driveway, we paused to admire the large villa in front of us. It was clad in pink marble imported from Italy at great expense by the original owner, Ambrose. I knew that he had made his fortune in vegetable peelers, but I hadn't realized exactly how profitable kitchen implements were until I saw this place.

As we walked up the carved marble steps, the front door swung open. Cassie greeted us, a martini glass in her hand.

"Mollie, Scooter, so good to see you," she said, slurring her words slightly. "And I see you brought your adorable cat with you."

"Do you mind?" I asked.

"No, not at all. We're in the drawing room. Follow me."

As we trailed behind her, I whispered to Scooter, "It's not even noon yet and I don't think that's her first martini."

"Everyone copes with grief differently," he whispered back.

When we reached the drawing room, Cassie whirled around. "What can I get you? Martini? Wine? Beer?"

"A glass of water or some coffee would be fine," I suggested.

"Lemonade? No problem." She sashayed over to a door on the opposite side of the large oak paneled room and stuck her head through. "Honey," she yelled. "Can you get some lemonade for our guests?" She turned back to us. "He makes the most delicious lemonade. Don't let the green color put you off. He adds in pureed kiwi fruit and honey. It makes it really sweet."

I nudged Scooter, asking in an undertone. "Who would she be calling 'honey'?"

He shrugged, then tried to shoo Mrs. Moto off an ottoman. She responded by rolling on to her back and demanding a belly rub.

"Have a seat," Cassie said, waving her arms around theatrically, the contents of her glass sloshing onto the thick Persian carpet. As we sank into the deep leather couch, she walked over to a bar in the corner of the room and topped up her glass. After plopping three olives in it, she sat on thé couch opposite us. "So, on the phone you said that you wanted to talk about the *Triviamania* auditions."

Scooter arched an eyebrow. "Auditions?" he mouthed.

"That's right," I said, ignoring Scooter's side eye at me. "We wanted to know more about how they were going to work. Are there any rules about what kinds of costumes you can wear?"

"Costumes?" Cassie kicked off her tennis shoes—bright red with cars embroidered on them—and tucked her legs underneath her. "No, you can wear anything you want. The more outlandish, the better I'd say. Viewers tune into see how crazily the contestants are dressed."

"I thought they watched the show, because of the trivia questions," I said.

"If you promise not to tell anyone, I'll let you in on a little secret." Cassie put her finger to her lips and made a shushing sound. "The people who watch *Triviamania* are dumber than rocks. But as long as they keep tuning in, the money keeps rolling in."

While she nibbled on one of her olives, I glanced over at Scooter. His mouth was agape. The woman who he admired had basically just called him an idiot.

"Here's the lemonade. Can you clear a place on the coffee table?" I looked up and saw the young man who had been locked in a passionate embrace with Cassie on *Factoid* holding a silver tray with a crystal pitcher and glasses. "Cassie, did you hear me? Can you please move your card making supplies out of the way?"

"Sure thing, honey," she said, looking at him with an adoring gaze. Then she swept a pile of colorful paper, stamps, ink pads, ribbon, and scissors onto the floor.

"Oops, can't lose that." She leaned down and picked up a gold pen. "This is a one of a kind, custom-crafted calligraphy pen. It's twenty-four carat gold. See the 'T' engraved on it? 'T' for *Triviamania.* I use it with a special ink. Now, where did that bottle go? Oh, there it is," she said, pulling it out from under a cushion. "See how it shimmers in the light? I had it blended especially for me. You won't find this shade of lilac anywhere else. I use it when I sign my name on personalized cards."

After Scooter and I admired the pen and ink, she looked at the young man and patted the empty spot on the table. "There you go."

As he set the tray down, his

expression darkened for a moment. Then he introduced himself, a warm smile on his face. "I'm Trevor Wallace. The caretaker of the estate."

"I hadn't realized that there was a caretaker until recently," I said. "How do you know Everett Hazelton?"

He chuckled as he poured glasses of lemonade and handed them to us. "It's a pretty boring story. And I'm sure you have more important things to discuss with Cassie."

Cassie held up her martini glass. "Trevor, honey, I need more olives."

"Sorry, I think those were the last of them."

She set her glass on the table and slipped her tennis shoes on. "Well then, I'll run out to the store and get some more."

As she started to get up, Trevor put his hand on her shoulder pushing her back down on the couch. "You can't drive anywhere in the state you're in," he said sharply. "You could kill someone. Could you live with yourself if you did that?"

"Nonsense," she said. "I'm fine."

"No, you're not. If you really want olives—"

She leaned against him. "I really, really do."

"Then, I'll go get them." The smile he gave her looked forced. After he extricated himself from her grasp, he excused himself. "Please, help yourself to more lemonade."

After he had left, I asked Cassie how she knew Trevor.

"He's a doll, isn't he," she said evasively. "I don't know what I'd do without him."

"He looks familiar," I said. "I think I saw him on your boat."

She furrowed her brow. "On *Factoid*? I don't think so. I've decided to sell her. She reminds me too much of Robert. Do you know any good boat brokers in the area?"

"Call Penny Chadwick," Scooter said calmly. "She'll do a good job for you."

I peered at my husband. He didn't seem to have any problem speaking to Cassie now. Finding out that your celebrity crush isn't anything like what you thought she'd be must be hard.

After Scooter gave Penny's number to Cassie, I tried again to find out more about her relationship with Trevor. "The two of you seem very close."

"Yes, we are. He really understands me."

"What is it that he understands about you?" I asked.

She dragged her fingers through her hair. "How stressful this business is. Do you know what it's like to have people constantly trying to get your autograph? Take pictures of you? The pressure to look good on television is intense. I hired Trevor to take care of public relations for me. My executive producer introduced us."

"But then why is he a caretaker here?"

"This is just a temporary situation. He'll start working for me full-time next month." She leaned forward. "Between us, Robert was livid when I told him about Trevor. But so what if he doesn't have any experience in PR. We all have to start somewhere, don't we?" She clapped her hands. "Well, let's talk about the auditions. I think we were discussing costumes?"

"Sure, but before we do, I heard that Chief Dalton came to see you yesterday. I was wondering if there was any update on the investigation. Do you have any idea who might have wanted to harm your husband?"

She frowned. "I know exactly who did it."

"Really?"

"Mind pouring me another one," she said, holding up her martini glass.

Scooter rolled his eyes, his celebrity

crush completely ... well ... crushed.

While I poured another martini for Cassie, Scooter went and sat next to Mrs. Moto on the ottoman, seemingly disinterested in continuing any conversation with the TV host. When I returned to the seating area, eager to find out who she had named as Robert's killer, I found Cassie with her head tipped back against the couch, snoring loudly.

CHAPTER 8
TRAWLERS VS. SAILBOATS

After our disastrous visit with Cassie Newton—we had watched her sleep for a half an hour before giving up and leaving—the rest of the week was unproductive in terms of the investigation. Chief Dalton was tight-lipped about pretty much everything— who Cassie had said killed her husband, if he was intending on making an arrest, and when he was planning on proposing to Anabel.

However, I did get some useful

information from Charmaine Buttercup. Apparently, the chief had been in a foul mood after he had gone to see Cassie, grumbling about how she had called him out to the Hazelton Estate only to tell him that she had a hunch who the killer was, but no hard evidence of any kind to substantiate her theory.

As the week wore on without Miguel being arrested, or even questioned further by the police, the Lopez family started to breathe a sigh of relief. Maybe the killer had been an outsider who had fled town, and the murder of Robert Ronaldo would remain an unsolved mystery.

While the investigation came to a standstill though, I was swamped with preparations for the protest march. The day after Scooter and I had seen Cassie at the Hazelton Estate, her lawyer had letters hand-delivered to the tenants of the Seaside Center. She had taken control of the premises and the letters confirmed that she intended to move forward with terminating their leases.

The tenants were more determined than ever to fight Cassie's plans to lease space at the shopping center to chain stores. Planning meetings were held each night at the Tipsy Pirate and by the time Saturday morning rolled around, the group was fired up.

We assembled at the far end of Main Street, near Melvin's Marine Emporium, all the tenants wore matching t-shirts which said, "Keep Coconut Cove Local." I marveled at how many people were gathered, ready to support the cause.

Somehow, a simple protest march had turned into a full-blown parade complete with the high school marching band and cheerleaders, the town's fire engine and ambulance, and representatives of various community groups including the library volunteers, the senior center, and the animal shelter. The local FAROUT chapter was out in full force and the floral society, led by Mrs. McDougal, had even constructed a float covered in roses.

"Isn't the turnout amazing?" Alejandra was grinning ear-to-ear. "With all the tourists in town for Labor Day weekend, our protest is going to get a lot of visibility. When Cassie sees the community support we have, she's bound to change her mind."

Anabel frowned. "Hopefully, she sees it. She's been holed up at the Hazelton Estate. No one has seen her around in days."

"Oh, I think we've got that covered," I said. "Penny's arranged to meet Cassie at the bandstand in the waterfront park. She'll have a front-row seat as the parade marches past her."

"How did she manage that?" Anabel asked.

"She wants to sell her trawler so they're meeting up to discuss the listing."

Ben and Scooter walked up to us holding "Keep Coconut Cove Local" signs.

"Who's selling their trawler?" Ben asked.

"Cassie Newton," I replied.

He scowled. "Good riddance to her and her stupid boat."

"Well, I'm not sure her boat is stupid."

"Of course it is," Ben said. "*Factoid* isn't a sailboat. You don't see a mast on it do you? No sails mean she's not a sailor. People who buy trawlers are either too old to manage a sailboat or too chicken to rely on sails rather than an engine."

Scooter frowned. "I don't know about that. From what I can tell, many of the people who own sailboats at the Palm Tree Marina seem to have their engines on most of the time.

"That's because they're fair weather sailors," Ben said.

"Says the man whose boat hasn't left

its mooring ball in years," I said dryly.

"Point taken," Ben said. "But, in any case, I don't like Cassie Newton any more. Scooter told me what she said about us being dumber than rocks."

Anabel said, "But you were just telling me about auditioning for *Triviamania*."

"Well sure. We're talking about being on TV. I'm not going to let my feelings about Cassie Newton get in the way of that." He lowered his voice. "Although, rumor has it that she might not be the host of *Triviamania* for much longer."

"Where did you hear that?" Scooter asked.

"From Brittany Abernethy."

"Did she say why?" I asked.

"No, it was a quick conversation. When I asked her if she wanted to go out for a drink later at the Tipsy Pirate, she said that she had to dash. Something about meeting up with her brother." He pointed across the street. "I suppose you could ask her highness herself why she's leaving the show."

Cassie Newton was standing next to the fire engine, having an intense conversation with Angus and Francine.

"Do you think they're convincing her not to terminate the leases?" Alejandra asked, clutching the scarf around her neck.

"I'm not sure," I said.

"Fingers crossed that's what's happening," she said then before rushing off to show the junior dance squad where they were supposed to be positioned.

Ben, Scooter, and I continued to watch Cassie's discussion with Angus and Francine. I tried to inch forward to hear what they were talking about. Only Scooter pulled me back, muttering something about eavesdropping not being a very ladylike trait.

"Oh, look," I said after a few minutes. "She just shook both of their hands. Maybe they've made some sort of deal."

"Yes!" Ben did a fist pump. "A deal to keep Coconut Cove local. So long Cassie Newton, don't let the door hit you —"

Before he could finish his thought, Francine and Angus approached us, their expressions grim.

"Um … sorry, but we're going to have to bail on the protest march," Angus said.

"Bail? Why?" Anabel asked.

Francine clutched her stomach. "Food poisoning, sweetie. I don't feel well."

"Yes, that's it. Food poisoning." Angus groaned while rubbing his belly. "We better get going. Don't want to get anyone else sick."

As they walked off, I shouted after them, "What exactly did Cassie Newton say to you?"

* * *

"Where are Francine and Angus?"

Alejandra asked me as I took my position in the parade line-up.

"They're not coming," I said. "After Cassie finished speaking to them, the both of them claimed that they had food poisoning."

"Food poisoning? Both of them?"

"It seems odd, doesn't it?"

"But I saw both of them eating donuts earlier." Her eyes grew wide. "Oh, no, do you think we all have food poisoning? Everyone here had donuts."

I shook my head. "I don't think they're really sick."

"But …" She scratched her head. "What? Are you saying that they're lying?"

"Yes, but the question is why. What did Cassie say to them?"

"This doesn't make any sense," Alejandra said.

"I know, it doesn't." I gestured at the large group assembled for the parade. "But given this incredible turnout, we won't miss a couple of people."

Anabel blew a whistle to get everyone's attention, issued a few last-minute instructions, then the marching band began to play.

Alejandra looked over at me. "This is going to work, I know it. Once Cassie sees all the support that we have, she's going to change her mind. She has to."

As we marched down Main Street waving our signs at the crowd, I tried to keep a smile plastered on my face. I didn't share Alejandra's confidence that Cassie was going to change her mind. Clearly there was something fishy going on and I didn't think it was in the tenants' best interests either.

By the time we reached the waterfront park, my mood had started to brighten, probably due to the enthusiasm of everyone around us, and the peppy tunes the band was playing.

However, my mood soured when I saw Chief Dalton talking to Alejandra's parents. Josefina looked pale and Eduardo looked shrunken. Both Alejandra and I rushed over to them.

"Mama, Papa, what's going on?" she asked her parents.

"The chief says that …" Eduardo switched to Spanish, his anxiety stripping away his ability to remember English.

"What do you mean the chief has arrested Miguel?" Alejandra stammered.

I looked at Chief Dalton. He returned my gaze and motioned for me to take a few steps away from the Lopez family.

"What's going on?" I asked him.

He took a deep breath. "Two witnesses approached me a little while ago. They're willing to testify that they saw Miguel shoot Mr. Ronaldo. I don't have any choice in the matter. I have to place Miguel Lopez under arrest."

CHAPTER 9
THE DISAPPEARING COOKIE

"Two eyewitnesses?" I had a sinking sensation in my stomach. "Let me guess. Their names are Francine and Angus."

"You know I can't confirm that," Chief Dalton said.

"It has to be them," I said. "I saw Cassie Newton speaking to them right before the protest march started. Then, out of the blue, the two of them suddenly came down with food poisoning. That seems a little too convenient, don't you think?"

"No comment."

"Do you think she bribed them to lie?"

"Again, no comment."

"Do you think Cassie told Angus that she wouldn't terminate his lease if he lied about seeing Miguel kill her husband?" I cocked my head to one side. "No, that doesn't make sense. If she was going to change her mind about one tenant, then wouldn't she change her mind about all of them? And we know she didn't do that, because she didn't speak with any of the other tenants."

The chief cleared his throat. "Mrs. McGhie—"

"Hang on a minute," I said. "You know what else doesn't make sense? Francine. She doesn't even own a shop at the Seaside Center. She works for Alejandra at the Nail Nook. Why would Cassie have singled her out to lie about Miguel? She wouldn't have even known her. It's not like she went into the nail salon for a manicure and met her that way. Or wait, did she?"

"Mrs. McGhie," Chief Dalton said impatiently. "I really don't have time for this."

"You're the chief of police. Investigating a murder should be your number one priority." I put my hands on my hips. "Especially when an innocent young man has been falsely accused."

"What I meant was that I don't have time to stand around here all day listening to your theories." He pointed at the Lopez family, who were sitting at one of the picnic tables. Eduardo had his arm around his wife. They both looked shell-shocked. Alejandra sat across from them, her head in her hands. Scooter was standing next to them, talking on his cell phone. "If you really want to help, you should make sure that Miguel Lopez has a good lawyer."

"I think Scooter is working on that already. What I need to work on is clearing Miguel's name." I pushed my shoulders back and flexed my fingers. "Cassie Newton obviously has some sort of incriminating information that she's holding over Angus and Francine's heads. Or she's promised them something too tempting to refuse. The bigger question is why she's doing this. My guess is that either she killed her husband or she's protecting the person who did it. Don't you agree?"

"No—"

I held my hand up. "Yes, I know—no comment. Listen, I don't have time to stand around here all day chatting with you. I have an investigation to conduct."

"An investigation," the chief spluttered.

"Uh-huh. Starting with her." I pointed at Francine, who was standing next to the public dock, holding a small boy's hand while he watched the fishing boats unload their catch. I started to walk away, then turned back around. "Hey, before I go, there was something else I wanted to ask you about."

The chief shook his head. "There's more?"

"Anabel told me you offered to have her engagement ring cleaned. Does that mean what I think it means?"

"It doesn't mean anything."

I grinned. "I think it does. You're going to propose to her again?"

"No comment," he muttered, looking down at the ground.

* * *

Francine looked wary when I approached her.

"Is this your grandson?" I asked, smiling at the boy who was now crouched down on the ground watching the seagulls fight over scraps of fish.

She gave me a curt nod, then averted her eyes. "Yes."

"What's his name?"

"Toby."

"How old is he?"

"Five," she replied brusquely.

I was perplexed. Usually, grandparents couldn't help but gush about their grandchildren, happy to answer your questions in great detail. Except Francine seemed reluctant to give me even one-word answers. At least the chief used two words when he was avoiding my questions—no comment.

Toby jumped to his feet. "I'm five-and-a-half, grammy."

"Five-and-a-half," I said, ruffling his hair. "You're a big boy, aren't you?"

He grinned, then twirled around, jabbing his hands in the air.

"Ouch." I grimaced as one of his punches landed on my leg.

Francine pulled him back. "Now, Toby, we talked about that. Real boxers don't punch people outside of the ring."

I rubbed my leg. "You're a boxer?"

"Uh-huh," he said, bouncing back and forth. "I'm gonna be a champion when I grow up, like Hoppin' Succotash."

"Hoppin' Succotash? Who's that?"

He grinned, a gap where his front baby teeth used to be. "Grammy talks about him all the time. He was the best northpaw ever."

Francine smiled affectionately at her grandson. "It's actually southpaw, honey."

"That's very impressive," I said, taking a stab that having paws were a good thing when it came to boxing. Mrs. Moto had paws—I wondered which one of hers was the north one and which one was the south one.

Toby hopped up and down. "He also knocked out—"

"Now, Toby, I'm sure Mollie doesn't want to hear about boxing." She grabbed the young boy's hand. "We need to get going. It's time for this one's nap."

"I bet you probably want to lie down too, considering you're not feeling well," I said.

"Are you sick, grammy?" Toby asked, tilting his head up to look at his grandmother.

"Uh-huh. Your grammy is really sick. She has food poisoning. That's why she wasn't marching in the parade today."

He squeezed her hand. "Is that true, grammy?"

Francine chewed on her lip. It seemed like she was torn about whether to lie or not to her grandson. Obviously, she didn't have the same qualms when it came to lying to the police.

"I had to watch you, pumpkin, since your mom is working," she finally said to him.

"Toby could have marched in the parade with you," I said. "There were lots of kids doing that."

"It was more fun for him to watch the

parade." She tugged Toby's hand. "Come on, time to go."

The young boy leaned against Francine's leg and sniffed. "My mom works all the time," he said quietly. Then, his mood changing abruptly, he hopped up and down again before darting off to watch the fishermen processing their catch.

Francine sighed. "It's tough being a single mom. You feel so guilty that you have to work."

"Were you a single mom too?" I asked.

"Yes, I raised my daughter on my own."

"Her father didn't help at all?"

"Help? Hah!" Francine said bitterly. "He wouldn't even acknowledge that she existed. Then he disappeared without a trace."

"I bet you did a great job raising your daughter on your own."

Francine's expression softened. "It wasn't easy, but she turned out great."

"As a mom, you'll understand what Josefina Lopez is going through right now. The police have arrested her son, Miguel."

Francine looked blankly at me. "Miguel?"

"You know exactly who I'm talking about. The guy *you* said killed Robert Ronaldo."

She furrowed her brow. "But I thought ..." her voice trailed off, then she crossed her arms over her chest and held my gaze. "I don't know what you're talking about."

"I think you know exactly what I'm talking about."

Francine scowled at me, then shouted, "Toby, come on, we're leaving now."

As she walked over to where the boy was standing, I called out, "Aren't you worried that your food poisoning is contagious? You don't want to get your grandson sick, do you?"

* * *

I watched as Francine dragged a very unhappy Toby away, then turned around to see if I could spot Angus anywhere. I doubted that he would be stupid enough to hang around after pretending to have food poisoning. He had probably skulked back to the chocolate shop to avoid any uncomfortable questions from his fellow tenants about his sudden illness.

I clenched my fists, anger bubbling up inside of me. How anyone could deliberately try to frame an innocent person for a murder was beyond me. What could possibly drive someone to do that? What could be worth that sort of deceit?

My phone buzzed. I took a deep breath and pulled it out of my purse. When I read the text from Scooter, I smiled.

Penelope is handing out free cookies.

I grabbed a couple of chocolate chip ones for you.

It was like the man sensed my mood and knew that chocolate would help.

Hurry up. The chocolate is melting.

I pushed my way through the crowd, finally spotting Scooter standing underneath one of the oak trees, nibbling on a cookie.

"Hey, is that one of mine?" I asked.

"No, this one is yours," he said, handing me a cookie wrapped in a napkin.

I pulled back the paper, took a bite, then said, "I thought you saved two cookies for me."

"Did I?"

"That's what your text said. Where did the other cookie disappear to?"

He wiped some chocolate off the side of his face. "Must have been a typo."

While I finished my treat, Scooter filled me in on the Lopez family. "I've arranged a lawyer for Miguel. Eduardo took Josefina back to the house to lie down. She has high blood pressure, and this situation isn't helping."

"What about Alejandra?"

"She's with the other tenants and Anabel over there." He indicated the group clustered around one of the picnic tables. "She wanted to go back with her parents, but they told her to stay here and find out if Cassie is going to change her mind about the lease. To be honest, I think being here is helping distract her from what's going on with her brother."

"Do we have any idea if Cassie is going to change her mind?" I asked. "She saw the parade, right?"

"Yep. She met Penny here at the park as planned and had a front-row seat as everyone marched in. But when I asked Penny about what Cassie's reaction was, she said that she was non-committal."

"Maybe that means she's mulling it over." I crossed my fingers, then clasped my hands together. "I wish we could find out what she's thinking."

"Maybe you could ask Brittany." Scooter pointed at the bandstand in the center of the park. The executive producer was pacing back and forth, talking on her phone.

"Hmm. I wonder what she's doing here," I said.

"Maybe she's scoping out the location for the *Triviamania* auditions."

"Are you still going to go to them?"

Scooter nodded. "Yep. Ben and I talked about it today. He told me about his costume."

"He's going as a pirate, right?"

"Yes, but not just any pirate."

"Let me guess—he's dressing up as Coconut Carl."

"You got it."

"And what are you going as?"

"It's a surprise." He smiled. "I also have an adorable costume picked out for you. You're going to love it."

"Me? I'm not auditioning."

"Of course you are," he said. "The whole Savvy Sailing Squad team is."

"Uh, I don't think so. It really isn't my —"

"Hold that thought," Scooter said. "It looks like Brittany is saying something."

The young woman waved her hands in the air. "Could everyone gather around, please? Cassie would like to say a few words about the Seaside Center."

Scooter and I walked over and joined the other tenants.

"What do you think she's going to say?" the florist asked.

"I bet she's decided to honor our leases," the bookstore proprietor said.

The deli owner chuckled. "Maybe she'll even lower our rents."

The florist's looked at him, wide-eyed. "Do you think so?"

"I doubt it," he said, shaking his head. "It'd be nice, but at this point, I'd just be happy not to have to shut down the deli."

"Shush," a man standing behind us said. "Cassie's on stage."

"She looks nervous, don't you think?" I whispered to Scooter.

He nodded. "It's not easy admitting you made a mistake."

Cassie pulled a piece of paper out of a red-and-white striped envelope, then looked briefly at the crowd before clearing her throat. She started to speak, but instead of the clear, authoritative voice that she had used when she had hosted the semi-finals at the Tipsy Pirate, her words were inaudible.

"Louder," someone shouted.

"Yeah, speak up," someone else said.

Another person yelled, "Keep Coconut Cove local!"

Brittany stepped forward and spoke in a loud voice that carried across the park. "If you could all quiet down, Cassie is going to read a prepared statement."

A hush fell over the crowd. Cassie smiled weakly. "First of all, I want to say how impressed I am with how many people turned out for this ... um ... parade. Coconut Cove is a very special town. That's why I'm excited to be the new owner of the Seaside Plaza." She toyed with the piece of paper in her hands. "Now, I wish that I could keep the old lease agreements in place, but —"

The crowd started booing.

"Keep Coconut Cove local!" the tenants chanted.

After a few moments, Brittany held up her hands for silence. "Please, let Cassie finish."

Cassie continued, "Except my late husband had already signed leases with new tenants." She put her hand to her heart. "Believe me, if it was up to me, I would reverse the decision. But unfortunately, I can't. However, I'm positive that the current tenants will be able to find new space to lease and that their businesses will continue to thrive."

She flipped the piece of paper over, scanned it, then looked back at the crowd. She whispered something to Brittany, then quickly walked off the stage.

Brittany fluffed up her tousled bob, then smiled brightly at the crowd. "Cassie and I wanted to remind everyone that *Triviamania* will be holding auditions right here at the waterfront park on Wednesday. I hope you'll all join us. And don't forget to wear a costume."

As Brittany hustled off the stage, ignoring the folks who tried to get her attention, Alejandra scowled. "Cassie Newton can stuff her auditions."

Other tenants chimed in with similar sentiments, some of them using more colorful language.

Then a quiet voice said, "If she's not

careful, she's going to be the next one to end up dead."

CHAPTER 10
NOCHOCOPHOBIA

The next morning, I sat in the cockpit of our sailboat watching how-to videos about going up a mast. They all seemed to feature young, fit people. Impossibly attractive guys and gals who didn't break into a sweat despite dangling sixty feet up in the air in the hot sun.

My stomach twisted in knots as I watched one man demonstrate how he performed the feat solo. I was on pins and needles as he scrambled up the steps attached to his mast. Would he make it to the top? If he fell, would his safety line really save him? What would happen if a flock of seagulls suddenly attacked him?

At one point, his foot slipped, and I thought he was a goner. I squeezed my eyes shut. When I didn't hear any screams of a man tumbling to his death, I resumed watching the video. The rest of it was anti-climactic. He got to the top, fixed an antenna, descended, then poured himself a beer.

I set my phone aside, grateful I wouldn't have to be part of this craziness. I remembered meeting a young woman named Ginny who had told me that being afraid of heights was called "acrophobia." I wasn't sure that my fear extended to phobia-territory, but glad that I wouldn't have to find out. The only phobia that I knew that I had was "nochocophobia"—the fear of running out of chocolate.

No, Scooter and Ben would do just

fine taking care of going up the mast by themselves. Fixing the marine toilet on our boat seemed like a piece of cake in comparison. Sure, it might be grosser, but you would be less likely to lose your life in the process.

I went down below to make some more coffee and check on Scooter. He had gone to bed early the previous night, complaining of a stomachache. I think it had to do with discovering more unpleasant facts about his celebrity crush and feeling conflicted about the auditions. He thought it had something to do with eating one too many cookies.

After I put the water onto boil, I poked my head into the aft cabin. He was sleeping peacefully, Mrs. Moto curled up beside him. Giving each of them a gentle kiss on their foreheads, I finished making my coffee drink—a mocha this time with extra chocolate syrup.

Grabbing my mug, I started to climb up into the cockpit, when I heard Cassie

Newton's voice. I carefully positioned myself at the top of the ladder, hunched over so that I couldn't be seen. Some people might argue that I was being nosy. Honestly, I wasn't. Eavesdropping is a legitimate investigative technique.

I sipped my coffee as I listened to Cassie's tirade.

"Are you kidding? That wasn't our agreement. If you think you can get away with this, you've got another thing coming. You know what happened last time someone crossed me."

I nearly dropped my mug when I heard that. It reminded me of that night in the Tipsy Pirate when she didn't realize that everyone was listening to her on the phone. She had threatened the other person on the end of the line, saying that the only way that—whatever 'that' was—would happen would be over that person's dead body. Not long after, someone had turned up dead, namely her husband.

I popped my head up a little bit to see what was going on. Cassie was leaning against her trawler, wearing an old t-shirt and leggings. Her hair was mussed, her eyes were puffy, and her face was makeup free. Yet, for some reason, she still looked amazing and years younger than her actual age, which I have to admit did make me feel a little jealous.

Trying not to think about how I looked every bit my age, I twisted my body slightly to get a glimpse of who she was speaking to. A man was standing next to her, his face obscured by the baseball hat he was wearing.

"We didn't agree to anything," he said.

"Yes, we did. I have a very clear recollection of our conversation at the Tipsy Pirate."

"So do I," the man said. "You tried to pay me off, and I refused."

"You took the envelope," she said.

"I didn't take it. You shoved it in my

pocket. Now I'm returning it." He turned slightly, removing his cap to wipe his brow before replacing it on his head.

I gasped. I knew I had recognized that tall frame and those broad shoulders. It was none other than Kyle Kaminski. He was holding the same red-and-white striped envelope that Cassie had passed him the night of the semi-finals.

As he tried to place it in her hands, she stepped to the side and folded her arms across her chest.

"Let's see if I have this right," she said. "Over a week ago, you happily took an envelope full of money. Now you want to return it?"

"Lady, I didn't take it. That's what I'm trying to tell you."

Cassie shook her head. "I wouldn't have done what I did, if you hadn't have taken the money. We had an agreement."

"We did not have an agreement," he said, throwing his hands in the air. "I was out of town for a few days on business. When I got back, I tried to track you down, but you were staying at that estate. I told the caretaker that I needed to see you, but he kept saying that you were indisposed."

She sneered at him. "Business. How can you call what you do business? It's a disgusting profession. People like you are worse than cockroaches. You're a blight on our society."

"Listen, I don't care what you think about what I do." He took a step forward, jabbing a finger in Cassie's direction. "It's an honest living." The tone of his voice didn't match his aggressive posture, almost as though he was trying to convince himself about what he did for a living.

"Honest? You destroy people's reputations, marriages, everything." Cassie started sobbing. I didn't buy it for one second. It was an Oscar-worthy performance.

Taking another sip of coffee, I wondered if either of them was capable of telling the truth.

Kyle laughed out loud. "Seriously, you can drop the pretense. I know exactly how you felt about your husband. You're glad to be rid of him. It suits you perfectly. Now you have complete control over his businesses. And now you can parade your boyfriends in public." He smirked. "Obviously after a suitable period of mourning."

"Fine," she said, her voice icy. "Perhaps we can come to another agreement. Perhaps a larger sum could induce you to reconsider our arrangement."

"There isn't anything you could offer me to make me change my mind." He waved the envelope in her direction. He held up the envelope and she took a step back. When she didn't take it, he tossed it on the deck of her boat.

"Fine with me." He pointed at the

envelope. "Better grab that before the wind blows it away."

As she rushed to grab it, Kyle walked down the dock, pulling his cell phone out of his pocket.

"It's done," he said to the person on the other end of the line. "And now we're done too."

* * *

Cassie grabbed the envelope, then went inside her boat. I finished my mocha while I thought about what I had overheard. Cassie had tried to pay Kyle off, but for what? Cassie did something that she wouldn't have done if Kyle hadn't taken the money, but what did she do? Kill her husband? And what exactly did Kyle do for a living that was worse than being a cockroach?

These questions weren't going to answer themselves. Clearly, I needed to go pay Cassie a visit on *Factoid*.

Etiquette said that I should go bearing a gift of some sort. Not only is it the polite thing to do, it makes the person you're visiting more likely to invite you in for a cup of coffee and a chat. Oh boy, did I have a lot of things that I wanted to chat with her about.

But what to bring? I looked around the galley first, but all I found was an empty box of cookies. Well, that's not exactly true. There was a lonely chocolate chip lurking at the bottom which I promptly popped into my mouth.

Poking around the main cabin, the only things that seemed remotely gift-worthy were some glitter pens and a set of *Star Wars* coasters. To be honest, I didn't want to give any of those up. Then a silver container on the table caught my attention. Everyone needs catnip, right? Cats enjoy it. Mrs. Moto loves rolling around in it, then after a few minutes of spastic activity, she gets a glazed look on her face and falls into a deep state of relaxation. Maybe it would have the same effect on humans.

After ripping the Purrtastic label off the container, I went over and knocked on *Factoid's* hull. "Hello, is anyone there?"

After a moment, Cassie peeked out from behind one of the curtains. I gave her a cheery wave. She gave me a half-hearted wave in return.

"Permission to come aboard?" I asked, waving the container in the air in what I hoped was an enticing manner.

She opened the door to the pilothouse. "It's Mollie, right?"

"Uh-huh." I pointed at *Marjorie Jane*. "Remember I live in the boat across from you. We visited you at the Hazelton Estate the other day too."

"Oh, sure," she said flatly. "Sorry, I'm feeling a little fuzzy. I've been having a hard time sleeping since I lost my husband so tragically."

I tapped the container. "I have the perfect solution for you. You sprinkle a little bit of this on your pillow and after a period of ... um ... intense energy, you'll fall right asleep."

"What is it?"

"It's an herbal remedy. Mind if I come on board?"

She nodded, leading the way down into her main cabin.

"Your boat is gorgeous," I said, admiring the brass port-lights and carved teak woodwork. "It's a shame that you're going to sell her."

Cassie picked up a cushion embroidered with mermaids and seashells and plumped it up. As she set it back down, she said, "I made some good memories here, but it's time to move on to new adventures."

"What kind of adventures?" I asked. "Something to do with *Triviamania*?"

"Kind of." She pointed at a pile of craft supplies on the table. "I'm starting a line of trivia-themed greeting cards. Robert thought it was a stupid waste of time, but now that he's gone ..." After sniffing and wiping away a few non-existent tears, she offered me coffee.

"Would you like it black or with some of my special creamer in yours?" she asked.

"I'll have what you're having."

After serving me, she sat down, leaning back against the embroidered throw cushions.

I took a sip, realizing instantly what made her creamer so special—booze. Pushing my cup aside, I tried to figure out what to start with—her recent visitor, what she had said to Francine and Angus, or where she was the night her husband was murdered. I decided to start with the topic that would be most recent in her memory.

"So, I saw Kyle Kaminski here this morning."

"Kyle who?"

"Tall guy, broad shoulders, good-looking." Before she could deny knowing him again, I quickly added, "I just saw you talking to him."

She inhaled sharply. "You heard us?"

"I was on my boat. The seagulls are really noisy around here, aren't they?"

Seemingly reassured by my non-answer, she took a sip of coffee. "Oh, Kyle. Yes, he came by to offer his condolences."

"That was nice of him. Is he a friend of the family?"

"Not exactly. My husband and he were business acquaintances."

I leaned forward. "I heard a rumor about Kyle. Maybe you can shed some light on it."

"I doubt it," she said. "I hardly know the man."

"You see, a friend of mine had been dating him. I'm concerned that he might be into some shady business dealings. But the problem is that I don't know exactly what he does for a living. I can't go to my friend and tell her to stop seeing him without some concrete information." I spread my hands open on the table. "Any information you can share would be really helpful."

Cassie scowled. "Kyle Kaminski is an awful man. He goes around sticking his nose in where it doesn't belong. Tell your friend to stop seeing him before she gets hurt."

"But what exactly does he do?"

"He's a ... hang on a minute, I hear my phone ringing."

While she went into the rear cabin, I examined the cards on the table. Each one was exquisitely decorated with stamps, embossment, decoupage, and stencils. On the inside were birthday-related trivia questions.

After I learned that more people celebrate birthdays in August than in any other month and that two billion birthday cards are sent every year, Cassie returned to the main cabin.

"The funeral parlor called," she said.

"They want pictures of Robert for the memorial. I had sent them a recent one that was taken, but they suggested that it would be nice to have some from various points in his life for the tribute board."

She dumped the contents of a shoe box onto the table, then shuffled through the old photographs, periodically holding one up to show me. "This was from when he was in the Army. See this one? It's from when he won Property Developer of the Year. Don't you love the dress I'm wearing? I bought it in Paris."

I tried to steer the conversation back to Kyle, but Cassie was focused on reminiscing about her life as a socialite in Chicago. "These are from a charity ball."

"Looks like it was a costume party," I said as she passed me a stack of photos. She seemed to favor elaborate outfits—Marie Antoinette, Little Bo

Peep, and Cleopatra. Robert must have been obsessed with sports. He had worn a football player's uniform, boxer, and golfer costumes.

She furrowed her brow as I flipped through them. "Some of those are from Halloween parties. Gosh, and some of those are really old photos from before we were married."

After showing me pictures of Robert and her with various politicians, she went into the galley. She poured herself another cup of a coffee with a rather large slug of her "special creamer" from a brown bottle. As she was screwing the lid back on, she knocked a white box off the counter.

"Oopsy-daisy," she said, picking it up and placing it on the table in front of me. "Want some chocolate?"

"This is from Angus Tanaka's shop, isn't it?" I asked.

"No idea. It was in Robert's briefcase. Brittany picked up his personal belongings from the police station for me. I was surprised she offered to get his stuff, to be honest."

"Why's that?"

"She couldn't stand Robert. I overheard her on the phone one day telling someone what a slimeball he was."

"Really? That must have upset you to hear someone bad mouthing your husband."

"Are you kidding? Robert was a slimeball. She was just telling the truth. I have no idea what happened between the two of them though. Maybe he made a pass at her." She chuckled, then pushed the box toward me. "Go on, help yourself."

While normally I never turn down chocolate, eating ones that had been at a murder scene was a step too far, even for me. "Um, that's okay. I had a big breakfast."

"Suit yourself." She took a sip of

coffee, then said, "It's odd that he had them. He hated chocolate."

"Maybe they were a gift for you," I suggested.

She snorted. "Hardly. He wasn't exactly the gift giving type."

I looked more closely at the box. It featured the new logo that Angus had designed with a Japanese bobtail cat surrounded by a tartan frame. When I had been at his shop the day after Robert's murder, Angus had told me that I had been the second person to get a box featuring the new logo. The first person had been the man who had been in trouble with his wife and thought chocolate and flowers might get him to forgive her.

How did Robert end up in possession of one of those boxes? It didn't make any sense at all. Had Angus given it to him? And if so, when did he see him—at his shop the evening of Alejandra's grand opening party or later that night on the trail by the beach?

Cassie slurped down the rest of her coffee, then yawned dramatically. She grabbed the can I had brought over, removed the lid, and sniffed the contents. "This smells wonderfully relaxing. Is there lavender in here?" Yawing again, she said, "You don't mind seeing yourself out, do you? I feel a nap coming on."

Then she promptly fell asleep, clutching the canister of catnip in her hand, leaving me with even more unanswered questions.

CHAPTER 11
A VERY GRUMPY CAT

I removed the canister of catnip from Cassie's hand, which took quite a few minutes as her fingers were clenched around it, then placed an afghan over her. She looked so peaceful as she slept. It was hard to believe that her husband had been recently killed, let alone that she might have had something to do with his murder.

After glancing again at the photos scattered on the table, and being momentarily tempted by the chocolates,

I headed back to *Marjorie Jane* where I was greeted by one very grumpy cat.

"What's wrong?" I attempted to stroke Mrs. Moto's head, but when she narrowed her eyes, I pulled my hand back.

She dropped a crumpled up piece of paper at my feet, yowled, then pushed it toward me with her nose.

"Oh, um, let me explain," I said, picking up the Purrtastic label. "I needed to borrow your catnip—"

The calico interrupted with something that sounded like a cross between a yowl and growl.

"But it was for a good cause," I protested. "It was for the investigation. And it worked. When Cassie saw that I came bearing a present, she invited me on board *Factoid*."

Mrs. Moto continued to express her displeasure, flattening her ears while she glared at me.

"I promise I'll get you some more

catnip." When that didn't seem to do the trick, I tried to appeal to her stomach. "Want me to open a can of Frisky Feline Ocean's Delight?"

She stopped glaring at me, but it was clear she wasn't anywhere close to forgiving me.

"Two cans?"

The growls subsided a bit, but from the look in her eyes, I could tell that she was holding out for more.

"Okay, final offer—three cans with smoked salmon on top."

That did the trick. She leaped into my arms, rubbed her face against mine, and purred loudly. My heart melted a little. When a cat decides that you're worthy of their affection, it's pretty rewarding, especially if they've made you work hard for it.

Then she decided it was time to eat, jumping out of my arms and bounding down below to the galley where her food was stored.

After piling an ungodly amount of food in a dish and setting it in front of Mrs. Moto, I checked in on Scooter.

When I entered the aft cabin, he rolled over onto his side and looked at me. "Is that smoked salmon I smell?"

"Did you want some on a toasted bagel with cream cheese? There's a little left."

"No, thanks." He clutched his stomach. "I'm still not feeling well. I don't think I'm going to be able to go up the mast today. Would you mind calling Ben and letting him know that I'll need to reschedule?"

"Sure," I said, kissing him on the forehead. "Why don't you try to get some more rest? I'll check in on you when I get back."

"Back? Back from where?"

"I have to run a few errands. We seem to be low on laundry detergent, and, uh, catnip. I also want to track Brittany Abernethy down."

Scooter eyes me suspiciously as he propped himself up on the pillows. "Why do you need to do that?"

"Because we're running out of clean clothes."

"Nice try. You know what I meant—why are you going to see Brittany? Please tell me this doesn't have anything to do with the investigation." He rubbed his temples. "I know I said I was okay with you looking into Robert Ronaldo's ... um ..."

"Departure?" I suggested, knowing Scooter's reluctance to use words like "murder," "killing," or "death."

"Yes, that. I know you're trying to help Miguel, but maybe you should leave things in Chief Dalton's hands this time."

"The chief is a busy man," I said. "I'm sure he'll be thrilled if I help out."

Scooter started chuckling, then rubbed his stomach. "Stop making me laugh out loud. It hurts my tummy. The last thing the chief will be is thrilled especially if you go around investigating things behind his back."

"I'm not doing anything behind his back. I've been sending him regular emails, giving him updates about what I'm doing. It's not my fault that he deletes them before reading them. Anyway, there's nothing to worry about. All I'm going to do is ask Brittany a few questions. I want to know more about Cassie Newton, and she probably knows more about her than anyone else in town."

Scooter seemed reassured by this reasoning. He probably would have been less reassured if I had told him what Cassie had said about Brittany having harbored ill-will toward Robert Ronaldo. Except when someone is sick, it's not a good idea to make them upset. I figured some things were better left unsaid.

I tucked his blanket around him, then gave him another kiss on his forehead before saying goodbye. As I turned to leave, I said over my shoulder, "You might want to check on Mrs. Moto later too. I have a hunch she's going to have an upset tummy later."

* * *

Before I left, Mrs. Moto made sure I understood what my number one priority was—buy more catnip before doing anything else—so my first stop was the Seaside Center. After purchasing all the containers of Purrtastic catnip that the pet store had in stock, I popped by the chocolate shop. I wanted to ask Angus how a box of chocolates with his newly designed logo ended up in Robert Ronaldo's briefcase. Though more importantly, I wanted to confirm if he in fact was one of the eyewitnesses that had come forward and, if so, what had caused him to tell such a blatant lie about the murder.

Also, I might have been having a serious craving for truffles.

Unfortunately, I was thwarted on all fronts by a "closed until further notice" sign on the door. It looked like I was going to have to be content with an old breath mint I found at the bottom of my purse instead of chocolate and answers.

After checking with some of the other tenants—no one had seen hide or hair of Angus since the day of the protest march—I waved at Alejandra as I walked past the Nail Nook. The salon was swamped with customers which was bittersweet. Business was obviously good, but the date when her lease would be terminated was looming. Add in what her brother was going through, and I was surprised that Alejandra could still function.

My stomach twisted in knots over what my friend was going through as I headed to the Honeysuckle Cottages, the bed-and-breakfast where Brittany was staying. Each white clapboard cottage bore a whimsical name, reflecting the owner's former career as a fortune teller. Vines bearing fragrant yellow flowers running wild over trellises, brightly painted doors, and stained glass windows added to the charm.

I found Brittany sitting on the porch in front of the "Crystal Ball" cottage, sipping on a glass of iced tea.

After I introduced myself, I explained that I lived on a boat at the marina.

"Are you staying here while you're working on your boat?" she asked. "The couple in the 'Tarot Card' cottage are doing that."

"That's the smart way to do it," I said. "Living on a boat while you're fixing it up is far from pleasant. Everything's torn up, tools strewn about, dirt, dust, and grease everywhere. It's a total nightmare."

Brittany grinned. "Tell me about it."

"You own a sailboat?"

"I've never owned one personally, but I sailed all the time on Lake Michigan with my parents. They did a complete overhaul of their last boat while still living on board. They were in the boatyard for almost two years. By the end of it, my mom was getting real tired of living without running water and having to climb up and down a ladder every time she had to go to the bathroom."

"My husband and I were in the boatyard for months." I shook my head. "I can't imagine having been stuck there for two years. Your mom sounds like a saint."

"She was." Brittany's eyes started to water. "All that work for nothing. They were almost done fixing the boat up when ..."

I cocked my head to one side. "What happened?"

"They were killed in a tragic accident."

She wiped at her face, then stiffened her shoulders. "There isn't a day that goes by that I don't miss them."

"I'm so sorry for your loss," I said. "Talking about sailboats must be a sad reminder of your parents."

"No, it's okay. Enough years have passed. It's actually a nice reminder of them. Sailing was something they were both incredibly passionate about. It's something I love too."

"Have you ever gone out sailing with Cassie Newton on her boat?"

"No. They always kept their boat down here in Florida. And it's not really a sailboat, is it? Trawlers have their nice attributes, but I'd take something with sails any day of the week over one of them."

"You live in Chicago, right?"

"Uh-huh. It's where we film *Triviamania*." She pointed at the laptop sitting next to her. "I'm actually working on selecting questions right now for the upcoming episodes we'll be taping in the next few weeks."

"I thought Cassie came up with all the questions on her own."

Brittany arched an eyebrow. "Hardly."

"Oh, I thought that's what my husband read in her autobiography."

"You shouldn't believe everything you read." She pressed her lips together while she fiddled with her necklace. "If it wasn't for me picking up the slack, she would have lost her job a long time ago. To be honest, I'm so tired of covering for her."

"Like what you did at the Tipsy Pirate during the semi-finals?"

"What do you mean?"

"When she walked onto stage and was yelling on her phone, you said that she was acting out a scene."

Brittany smiled faintly. "You didn't buy that excuse?"

"I think most people did. But they're huge Cassie Newton fans."

"I'm guessing you're not." I shook my head. "Well, you're in the minority. Most people think she's the best thing since sliced bread."

"You must think she's great, though," I said. "You're the executive producer of her show."

"I'm the executive producer of *Triviamania,* not of *her* show.*"

"What's the difference?"

"The network can always hire a new host."

"I've heard some rumors that she might be leaving," I said, remembering what Ben had told me.

"Things don't stay quiet for long in this industry. And there's a limit to what they'll put up with."

"Do you mean her drinking? It seemed like she had a few drinks that night at the Tipsy Pirate."

"Oh, you noticed that too," Brittany said. "Not a lot gets past you, does it? Well, between you and me, she's always had a drop or two of liquid courage before taping—she's actually quite shy—but lately, she's been drinking a lot more. She's been flubbing her lines. I can't even begin to tell you how many times we've had to stop shooting in order for her to get her act together."

"Wow, what do you think is going on? There must be a reason that she's drinking more."

"Not my business," she said. "I try to stay out of her personal life."

"What about her husband's personal life?"

She frowned. "Her husband?"

"Cassie told me that you couldn't stand him."

"I have no idea why she would say that. I hardly knew the man." She shook her head. "That was probably the booze talking."

"But I saw you speaking with him at the Seaside Center the night of the nail salon's grand opening."

"Did I?" She took a sip of her tea. "Oh, yes, now I remember. I saw him there that night talking with some guys. They all looked pretty hot under the collar— shouting something about their leases— so I thought I'd rescue Robert. I walked him to his car and said goodnight. See what I mean about Cassie and her drinking? If I hated her husband, would I have helped him out that night?"

"I guess not." I furrowed my brow. "But what were you doing there that night, anyway?"

Brittany held up one of her hands. "Making an appointment for a manicure. I need to get these touched up and I won't be back in Chicago for a few weeks."

"You mentioned how Cassie's drinking was interfering with her job. Do you think it could have led her to do something, um, more drastic?"

"Drastic?"

I smoothed down my *Star Wars* t-shirt while I tried to figure out how to frame my next question. After a moment, I blurted out, "Do you think Cassie killed her husband?"

Brittany almost dropped her glass, then spluttered, "Killed her husband? But they already have the killer in custody."

"Alleged killer," I said. "I have it on good authority that Cassie was having an affair. What if her husband had found out about it and threatened to divorce her? What if she decided she'd rather be a widow instead? Maybe that would have been more beneficial for her financially?"

"An affair? Are you sure?"

"Positive."

Brittany took another sip of her tea. "That's interesting."

"You don't seem surprised."

"I guess I'm not. I've learned things about her lately that made me realize I never really knew her at all." Brittany took a deep breath, then exhaled slowly. "Maybe you're right. Maybe Cassie is a killer. She thinks she's smarter than everyone else. She probably thought she could get away with it."

"What do you think she'd do if she thought the police were on to her? Do you think she'd try to bribe people to lie about who did it?"

Brittany nodded slowly. "That sounds exactly like what she'd do. And it wouldn't be the first time either."

* * *

When I asked Brittany what she meant about it not being the first time that Cassie had bribed someone, she clammed up, stating that I had misunderstood what she had said. I tried to press her some more, but she told me she had a video conference call. She grabbed her laptop and hurried into her cottage, leaving her phone sitting on the porch railing. I picked it up and knocked on the door. Opening the door slightly, she mouthed that she was on a call, then quickly pulled the door shut.

I looked at the phone in my hand and sighed. Why is it that people like to drop bombshells—like so-and-so bribes people, so-and-so is a killer, or so-and-so uses carob chips instead of chocolate chips in their cookies—and then refuse to elaborate on the matter?

I hated to do it, but it was time to enlist Chief Dalton's support. To my mind, the case against Cassie Newton was stacking up, but I was at a dead end.

Placing Brittany's phone back where I found it, I called the police station to ask if the chief was available. Charmaine Buttercup answered the phone.

"Sorry, honeybunch, he's tied up all morning. He won't be free until after lunch. Speaking of lunch, do you want to grab a bite at the Sailor's Corner Cafe with me? The chief said that their apple pie is to die for."

I chuckled. "He might have it confused with the peach."

After arranging a time to meet, I thought about the case against Cassie. Two questions stood out in my mind— where was Cassie the night of the murder and what was her exact financial situation. The first question was key—if she had an alibi for that night, then I'd have to consider other suspects, namely Angus. Not only did he have a strong motive, there was also that box of his chocolates that was in Robert's possession the night he was murdered.

Of course Cassie's boyfriend, Trevor, could have done it on her behalf. I groaned and put my head in my hands. Why was this case so complicated? I remembered what Anabel had said about there being a private investigator in town that hadn't bothered to check in with the chief. Did private investigators have a tough time with their cases? If only I knew who the private investigator was, maybe I could pick their brain.

While I was pondering this, Brittany darted out of her cottage, grabbed her phone and rushed back inside. I shook my head, then headed to the rose garden to kill time until Charmaine would be free for lunch. Mrs. McDougal was there planting some new "Celebration Rose" bushes. While she added some bone meal to the soil, she complained to me about how many people were breaking the rules in the new garden.

"Did you know I even caught some kids skateboarding here? They spoil it for everyone," she said. "And what's even worse, they could seriously hurt someone if they crashed into them."

After promising her that I'd keep an eye out for any offenders in the future, I made my exit and headed to the Sailor's Corner Cafe.

"Sorry, I'm late," Charmaine said as she slipped into the seat across from me a few minutes after I got there. "I had to take care of a really weird request from the chief before I left."

"Related to the murder?"

"No, at least I don't think so." She pulled the menu toward her and flipped it open. "He wanted me to see if I could find an Elvis costume for him."

"Yeah, that's definitely not related to the investigation." I grinned and slapped the table with my hand. "I knew he'd go through with it."

"Go through with what, honeybunch? Is he hosting a costume party? Ooh, I hope so. Dale and I love costume parties. One year we went as Tarzan and Jane. There was a freak snowstorm and I froze my patootie off, so the next year we went as Arctic explorers. We wore these cute fur-trimmed parkas and boots. Fake fur, mind you. I'm a vegan, you know."

She pulled out her phone. "Maybe I have a picture on here somewhere. Anyway, I was so hot in that costume. Sweat was dripping everywhere, and I mean everywhere, if you know what I mean ... Oh, here you go. See how my mascara's running down my cheeks?"

While I flicked through the pictures, Charmaine continued to tell me about all the costume parties she and her husband had attended over the past two decades. I was surprised that she had time to do anything else in her spare time.

"This is one of my favorite ones." She pointed at a photo of her wearing a sequined ice skating costume. "I borrowed this from a friend of mine. She placed third in the regionals wearing this exact same outfit. I won first prize that year."

It wasn't until the waitress asked Charmaine for her order—a veggie burger and tater tots—that I was able to get a word in edgewise.

"What else did the chief say?"

"About dressing up as Elvis? Nothing. Where's he having the party? Here at the cafe? I heard they have an event room in the back."

"I don't think there's going to be a party," I said. "I think he has something entirely different planned."

"Ooh, that sounds mysterious. What is it?"

"I'd love to tell you, but this is one secret I have to keep. One thing I can promise is that if his plan works, he'll keep trimming his eyebrows."

"Does he really trim them?" Charmaine asked as she stirred five packets of sugar into her coffee. She took a cautious sip, made a face, then added two more packets. "What did they look like before?"

"Imagine two woolly caterpillars on steroids taking up residence on his forehead."

"Wow, that bad?" I nodded. "And now he trims them. Hmm ... let me guess, there's a woman involved."

"There is. She's a good friend of mine."

"Well, if he's dressing up like Elvis to impress her, he's on the right track. One year, Carl wore an Elvis costume, and, boy, did he look handsome. I told him that he should—"

The waitress dropping off our food caused Charmaine to lose her train of thought. After she squirted half a bottle of ketchup over her tater tots, she looked up at me. "Did I mention what happened right before the chief was supposed to leave for a meeting?"

I took a bite of my grilled cheese and shook my head.

"This chief was in the lobby handing me some files when this guy rushed in. He had his head down, talking on his phone, and wasn't looking where he was walking. He ended up barreling into the chief, knocking him down on the floor. Let me tell you, the chief wasn't happy about that. He snapped at the guy, telling him to look where he was going."

Charmaine speared some tater tots with her fork, swirling them around in the ketchup.

"Was that it?" I asked, waiting for some sort of segue into costume parties.

"Oh, no, I'm just getting to the best part." She held up her finger to indicate that her mouth was full. Then she dropped a bombshell. "The man said that Cassie Newton confessed to killing her husband."

Fortunately, once she finished the rest of her lunch, Charmaine elaborated on what had happened. Pushing her plate to one side, she leaned across the table. "It was that friend of Cassie Newton's, the caretaker of the Hazelton Estate. He said that she got really drunk, then admitted that she had killed her husband, because she was afraid he was going to divorce her. And here's the really interesting part—she tried to bribe him into keeping what she did a secret."

CHAPTER 12
SCHRÖDINGER'S CAT

I wasn't sure what was worse—the fact that Cassie Newton was walking around free or the costume I was wearing. Trevor had gone into the police station on Sunday and told Chief Dalton that Cassie had confessed to killing her husband. It was now Wednesday evening, and she still hadn't been charged with murder.

On a more positive note, Miguel was no longer a person of interest. According to Charmaine Buttercup—

who swore me to absolute secrecy—when the chief dug deeper into Angus and Francine's accounts of seeing Miguel shoot Robert Ronaldo, they both fell apart, admitting that Cassie had pressured them into lying.

What Charmaine didn't know was what was going on with Cassie. She had come into the station for questioning, accompanied by several lawyers. A few hours later she walked out complaining about how awful the coffee tasted. Charmaine was slightly offended by this, considering she was the one who brewed it.

"What are you supposed to be dressed as, sugar?" Penny tapped my shoulder, interrupting my thoughts.

I turned, smiling when I saw her mermaid costume. She twirled around slowly so I could admire the iridescent sequins adorning the tail. Her long blonde hair cascaded down her back, fake seaweed woven throughout it.

Around her neck was a seashell choker.

"I wish I was wearing something like that instead of this," I said.

"And what exactly is this?"

"I'm a qutrit."

She furrowed her brow. "A what, sugar?"

"I don't know how to explain it," I said. "It was Scooter's idea."

"What was my idea?" Scooter asked as he came up behind me and wrapped his arms around my waist. Then he pulled back, staring at his thumb. "That hurt. One of your safety pins pricked me."

While I refastened the pin, Penny looked back and forth between the two of us. "Let me see if I can figure this out. Mollie has a large pompom attached to her shirt."

Scooter nudged me. "See, I told you people would get it."

Penny looked around her playfully. "I'm not sure who here gets it, but it sure isn't me."

"But you see the numbers on the top of her shirt, don't you?"

"The numbers one, two, and three. Yep, I see them. But it still doesn't make it any clearer."

"Okay, let me demonstrate." As he unpinned my pompom, it separated into three smaller pompoms.

"So, this is like a magic trick?" Penny asked.

"A really nerdy magic trick," I muttered as Scooter pinned one of the smaller pompoms under the number one, another under the number two, and the final one under the number three.

"Ta-da!" Scooter grinned. "Each of the pompoms represents a piece of quantum information which can simultaneously be in the positions one, two, and three."

Penny rubbed her temples, like she was getting a headache. I can't say that I blamed her. I had already taken several pain relievers and was wondering how many hours I needed to wait until I could pop a few more pills.

"You get it now, don't you?" Scooter asked Penny eagerly. "She's a qutrit. Did you know that physicists have been able to teleport them?"

"No, I sure didn't," she said politely.

"In fact, she's my little qutrit." Scooter kissed me on my cheek, then grinned. "That's my new pet name for you, 'my little qutrit.'"

I groaned. "No, please, not a nerdy, physics-related name. I don't want to have to explain it to everyone multiple times."

"That won't be a problem. Just demonstrate using your costume."

"I might be sorry that I asked this," Penny said. "But what are you dressed as, Scooter?"

He tucked his black t-shirt into his black jeans. "A black hole."

"It seems like you got off easy," she

said.

"Hey, I'll have you know that a lot of thought went into this outfit. I had to go out and buy black flip-flops."

"Wait until you see Mrs. Moto's costume," I said. "She's dressed as Schrödinger's Cat."

"Finally, a costume I can understand," Penny said.

"You know what Schrödinger's Cat is?" I asked.

"I assume it's something like Cat Woman."

"Close enough," I said.

Scooter cleared his throat. "We should get going. The auditions are starting soon."

We walked toward the parking lot at the marina—a slow process because when a member of your party is wearing a mermaid tail, they can only take small steps. I asked Penny what had happened to Cassie Newton's boat, *Factoid*.

"When we got up this morning, it was no longer docked across from us."

"She took it to the public docks at the waterfront park," Penny explained. "She's going to use it as her dressing room for the auditions."

"I still can't believe they're letting her host *Triviamania*," I said.

"Hopefully, it won't be for long," Scooter said. "If what I read online is true, the network is negotiating an exit agreement with her. That's the only reason I'm still auditioning. She's going to be history, but *Triviamania* will continue on."

"It's hard to believe you had a huge crush on her just a week ago," I said.

Penny I exchanged glances while Scooter huffed. "I never had a crush on her."

After getting into the car—easier said than done for Penny with her mermaid tail—we drove to the waterfront park. The place was packed with people wearing costumes. Cute costumes that you could understand at a glance and didn't require a science demonstration.

"Alejandra and Ben should be around here somewhere," Penny said. "You're tall, Scooter. Can you see them?"

"They're over by the bandstand talking to Chief Dalton," he said.

"The chief's here?" I stood on my tip-toes, trying to catch sight of him. "Is he wearing an Elvis costume?"

"No," Scooter said. "Just his regular police uniform."

I started to elbow my way through the crowd. "Come on, you guys."

"Wait for us, my little qutrit," Scooter called out.

I didn't wait around for the two of them though, running as quick as my short little legs could manage. I needed to catch the chief before he did another disappearing act on me. He certainly wasn't answering my phone calls or responding to my emails. This was the only chance I was going to get.

By the time I reached him, I was panting and sweat was dripping down my face onto my pompoms. While I caught my breath, the chief looked at my costume. "I probably shouldn't ask this, but what are you supposed to be, Mrs. McGhie?"

"It's complicated," I said. "Whatever you do, don't ask Scooter to explain it."

"Okay. I was just leaving anyway."

"Not before you answer a few questions." As I took a step forward, one of my pompoms fell on the ground.

Alejandra picked it up and handed it to me. "It's okay. I already asked him for an update on the investigation."

"You did?" She nodded. "And he gave you one?"

"Well, kind of."

"Let me guess. He said, 'no comment.'" I jabbed my finger in the chief's direction. "Listen, we deserve a better explanation than that. Cassie

Newton could be a killer and she's running around loose. We could all be in danger here."

"The only thing you're in danger of, Mrs. McGhie, is losing more of your costume." He pointed at another wayward pompom on the ground.

Ben retrieved this one for me, spearing it with the sword from his Coconut Carl costume.

Alejandra tugged my arm. "Come on, Mollie. The auditions are starting. We need to get seats."

"You two go ahead while I finish up with the chief. Take them with you." I pointed at Scooter and Penny, who were stuck behind a large family dressed as penguins.

To my surprise, the chief didn't try to escape. I had anticipated him trying to beat a hasty exit, while muttering "no comment." Instead, he removed his hat and scratched his head.

"Mrs. McGhie ... Mollie ... can I ask

you something without you blabbing it to everyone?"

"Of course. Your secret is safe with me." I pretended I was locking my lips with an imaginary key.

"Normally, you'd be the last person I'd ask—"

"Gee, thanks."

"But you're Anabel's closest friend." The chief took a deep breath, then quickly said, "Do you think she would like to go to Chez Poisson?"

I clapped my hands together and jumped up and down. "Is that how you're going to do it? A fancy dinner followed by a proposal?"

The chief held up his hand. "I never said I was going to propose. It's just dinner." After a beat, he added, "So? Would she like that?"

"Tell you what. You tell me what's going on with Cassie Newton, then I'll answer your question."

The chief shook his head. "Like I said,

you don't need to worry about her."

"Are you saying she didn't do it?"

"No—"

I didn't even bother to let him finish. We both knew what he was going to say. "How can she be innocent? She bribed Angus and Francine to lie about Miguel. According to Brittany Abernethy, it's not the first time Cassie has done something like that."

"Mrs. McGhie—"

"Don't bother. I know what you're going to say. No comment."

He shook his head. "No, I was going to say that you lost another pompom."

"These qutrits are really getting on my nerves," I said.

"Qutrits?"

"Something to do with quantum entanglement. I really hope there are some physics trivia questions during the auditions. It's all Scooter has been studying lately. It's sweet, really, how much he wants to get on the show."

I smiled as I thought about how adorable my husband was with his newfound obsession with physics. It sure beat his old one with Cassie Newton. Then I looked at the chief, standing there, hopelessly in love with his ex-wife. Obviously, he was desperate to propose to her again, but not sure how to do it.

"Anabel would love dinner at Chez Poisson," I said. "Actually, I know for a fact that she'd love dinner anywhere with you."

The chief's face reddened. "Really?"

"Really."

He put his hat back on his head, then leaned down and whispered in my ear. "Cassie has an air-tight alibi." Then, after dropping that little bombshell without further explanation, he walked off humming an Elvis tune.

* * *

"Ladies and gentlemen, can I have your attention, please?"

Brittany was standing on the bandstand stage, looking like a natural holding the microphone. Her hair, makeup, and casual chic outfit were camera ready, and she seemed to be feeding off the energy of the crowd. I wondered if she had aspirations to become the new host of *Triviamania* once Cassie was finally ousted.

Most of the audience fell silent, except the family of penguins, who chattered among themselves while taking selfies.

The young woman walked to the center of the stage and smiled brightly. "How about we have a warm-up question? What is the only species of penguin that ventures north of the equator in the wild?"

That got the selfie-obsessed family's attention. Jumping up and down, and waving their flippers in the air, they all screamed in unison, "The Galapagos

Penguin!"

"Very good," she said. "We're going to begin the auditions shortly. Here's how it's going to work. We'll call two teams up at a time. They'll go head-to-head, with the winner going on to the next round."

I eyed up our rivals, the Barnacle Babes Brigade. I knew the captain of their team was hoping for a rematch with us after their disastrous performance the previous week at the Tipsy Pirate. It was crazy how competitive people could get over trivia contests.

After scanning the rest of the crowd to see if there were any other teams that I needed to worry about, I focused my attention back on Brittany.

"The host of *Triviamania* ..." she paused, looking like she had just swallowed something unpleasant. Plastering a smile back onto her face, she continued, "Our host, Cassie

Newton, will ask each team a series of questions from random trivia categories. If you know the answer, press your buzzer."

"Now, here's where it gets tricky. When we're deciding who to send to Chicago for the next round of auditions, we take into account more than just your trivia knowledge. We're also looking for enthusiasm and creative costumes. So when you're up on stage, make sure you bring your A-game."

Scooter squeezed my hand. "With our costumes, we're a shoo-in."

I wasn't sure that his black t-shirt, black jeans, and black flip-flops, let alone my pom-poms, were going to earn us any points. Despite that and not wanting to dampen his enthusiasm, I squeezed his hand back and said, "Go, Savvy Sailing Squad."

Ben heard me and chimed in. "Savvy Sailing Squad, Savvy Sailing Squad!"

Alejandra, Penny, and Scooter joined

in. Soon there were competing chants from other teams, and the din of the crowd became deafening.

A loud noise crackled over the speakers as Brittany tapped her microphone. Everyone grew quiet, except the penguin family who continued to chant, "Go, Aptenodytes! Go, Aptenodytes!"

It actually made for an awkward chant, unless you happened to know that "Aptenodytes" refers to the genus that includes Emperor and King penguins. If you did, then you thought it was cool in a geeky way. If you didn't, you would think that they sounded like they were sneezing in a foreign language.

After realizing that everyone was staring at them, the penguin family finally piped down.

Brittany motioned at the audience. "Love the enthusiasm! Now, let's hear you cheer for the host of *Triviamania*, our very own Cassie Newton."

The theme music blared from the loudspeakers, the crowd clapped, and Brittany turned and looked expectantly at the path which led from the public docks to the bandstand.

When Cassie didn't appear, Brittany pursed her lips. She conferred with a harried-looking assistant, then turned back to the audience. "Sorry about that, folks. Apparently, Cassie is at the sports pavilion checking out your adorable pets. She'll be with us shortly."

"Is that where Mrs. Moto is?" Ben asked me.

"Uh-huh," I said. "They decided to set up a spot where people's pets can wait during the first part of the auditions. They thought it would be a bit chaotic to have all of them out here right now. They'll bring them up on stage later to show off their costumes. The couple who own the pet store are taking care of them."

Scooter looked at me. "Maybe we

should go check on her. I'm worried she might have done something to her box."

"Her box?" Penny asked.

"It's part of her Schrödinger's Cat costume," Scooter said. "You put a cat inside a box—"

"Cats love boxes," Penny said.

"We're using a cardboard one," Scooter said. "Schrödinger's thought experiment involved a steel box and radioactive—"

"I'll go check on her," I said, interrupting his explanation. I had heard way too much about Schrödinger and his cat over breakfast. "You stay here with the rest of the team. You're the captain, after all."

"Yes, but we all know who's really in charge," Ben said. "It's the admiral, Mrs. Moto."

After checking on Mrs. Moto—she had managed to remove her box and was now napping inside it—I walked back toward the bandstand. Angus Tanaka was sitting on a bench across from the public docks, staring forlornly at the boats sailing in the bay. He startled as I sat next to him.

"Mollie, what are you doing here?"

"I'm here for the *Triviamania* auditions. What are you doing here? Shouldn't you be at your shop?"

He ran his fingers through his unruly red hair. "I can't bear to go back there."

"Is that because you feel guilty?" I asked coldly. "I bet that's why. You lied about seeing Miguel Lopez shooting Robert Ronaldo, and now you're too embarrassed to be anywhere near the Seaside Center in case you run into Alejandra."

"I've already told the chief that I misspoke when I said that I had seen Miguel." Angus averted his eyes, then lowered his voice. "Do you think Alejandra will ever forgive me?"

"Misspoke? Is that what you call it?" I pressed my lips together. "That's a term that people use when they're too cowardly to admit that they lied."

"You're right," he said. "I need to apologize to her and her family, but I don't know how to go about it."

"It's better to do it now," I said, a much gentler tone to my voice. "The longer you leave it, the harder it will be. And you're in luck. Alejandra is here today."

"She's not at her nail salon?"

"No, she left one of the nail technicians in charge."

Angus smiled wryly. "I don't suppose it was Francine."

"No way. As soon as Alejandra heard the rumor that Francine was one of the eyewitnesses, she confronted her. Francine still wouldn't admit it, but it was obvious that it was her. Alejandra wouldn't let it go and Francine finally quit. She said some pretty nasty things to Alejandra before she left, telling her that she had no idea how to run a nail salon and that she'd always be a failure."

Angus frowned. "No way. From what I've seen, Alejandra knows exactly what she's doing."

"She sure does," I said. "I was glad she was able to get one of the girls to cover for her. She wanted to be here for the auditions. Although, I have to say I was surprised she decided to come, knowing that Cassie Newton would be here. But she said that it's better to face your demons personally, rather than hide from them."

Angus nodded. "Point taken."

"Why did you do it?" I asked bluntly. "What did Cassie bribe you with? Or was it blackmail?"

"I can't talk about it. Let's just say that she knew what my soft spot was ..." his voice cracked as he shifted on the bench. "Tell Alejandra that I'll speak to her later. Right now, I'm going back to my shop. There are some things I need to take care of there."

I watched as he slowly walked away, his head hung low and his shoulders slumped.

Leaning back against the bench, I texted Scooter to tell him I'd be back shortly, then looked at *Factoid*. The blue trawler was tied up at the public docks next to a fishing charter boat. Was Cassie on board? She hadn't been at the sports pavilion when I was there checking on Mrs. Moto, and the pet store owners said that they hadn't seen her turn up either.

I texted Scooter again, asking if Cassie was on stage.

No. They're roaming through the audience interviewing teams now. Think they're killing time until she shows.

I sent a message back, saying that I'd look for her on board *Factoid*.

A pair of orange tennis shoes was sitting on the dock next to her boat. They were decorated with colorful question marks—perfect for the host of a trivia show. I knocked on the hull, but when I didn't get a response, I hesitated. Boat etiquette dictated that you didn't go on board someone else's boat without an invitation. There were exceptions to this rule—like if the boat was in danger of sinking, for example.

I took a step back and looked at the trawler. She did look like she was listing to starboard, leading me to believe that some sort of sea monster had chewed a hole in that side of the hull. Water was probably rushing inside the bilge while Cassie was embellishing card stock, completely unaware of the imminent danger she was in.

Of course, Scooter would have probably said that the reason the boat was listing to one side was because she was unevenly weighted. He'd even say that it could be that the diesel and water tanks were all on the starboard side. Or the owners had all of their canned goods and cases of beer stored on one side. Sure, that was probably the more logical explanation, but what if sea monsters had been involved? What if I did nothing and water flooded into the main cabin?

No, I had to do something. So like any Good Samaritan would do, I quickly climbed on board and dashed down below. Surveying the scene, I realized that the boat was completely dry, that is except for the puddle of liquid on the floor. I quickly traced the source of the liquid—an empty bottle of vodka teetering from the edge of the table.

She was slumped next to the bottle, greeting cards and card making supplies scattered around her. I bet Brittany was furious. Cassie was drunk again, ruining the taping of the *Triviamania* auditions. Or maybe she wasn't furious at all. She might be thrilled—one last nail in Cassie's coffin, so to speak. The higher-ups at the network might decide this was the final straw and fire Cassie on the spot.

"Cassie, Cassie, wake up," I said, shaking her gently. "Come on, get up. I didn't wear this stupid costume for nothing. Time to get this show on the road."

As I shook her again, her head rolled to one side. The muscles in her face were all slack, her eyes were vacant too. I felt for a pulse, but I knew that I wouldn't find one. Cassie wasn't going to be hosting *Triviamania* ever again.

CHAPTER 13
NO LOVE LOST FOR POODLES

While I waited for the police to arrive, I had a closer look at the greeting cards scattered on the table. Each of the original trivia facts on the inside of the cards had been crossed out with a thick red pen, and underneath someone had used a combination of stickers, stencils, and stamps to add new questions and answers.

As I read through them—being careful not to touch anything—I noticed that they all had a boozy theme:

What did Paul Revere have before his famous ride? Two drinks of rum.

How many bubbles does the average bottle of champagne have? Forty-nine million.

What is the oldest brewery in the United States? Yuengling.

How do you turn a martini into a Gibson? Add a miniature onion to it.

The final card I looked at had a more chilling and personalized question:

Which television host deserves to die for what she did?

I gulped as I read the answer—*Cassie Newton.* Then a shiver ran down my spine as I realized what this meant. Cassie's death wasn't accidental. Someone thought she had deserved to die, and they made sure that it had happened too.

I examined the card more carefully. Unlike the other ones, the answer to this question had been handwritten with a calligraphy pen using a shimmering lilac ink. It looked like the same color of ink that Cassie had shown me when Scooter and I had paid her a visit at the Hazelton Estate. She had bragged about the ink having been blended especially for her. Did that mean that Cassie had written her own name on the card before she was killed? Or had someone written it for her, someone who had access to her special ink?

The boat rocked back and forth as someone boarded it. I quickly took photos of the greeting cards, then stepped back and took a picture of the larger crime scene. That's when I noticed pills strewn about on the floor next to a glass half-full with a green liquid.

Before I could bend down to inspect them more closely, a deep voice called out. "Are you down here, Mrs. McGhie?"

The burly chief of police made his way down into the main cabin, followed by two other police officers. As they all tried to maneuver around each other—not easy inside a boat—the chief ordered me to wait outside on the dock.

I texted Scooter to let him know what was going on, carefully avoiding words such as "murder," "dead body," "death threat," and "killer." The one word I didn't need to avoid using was "blood," because there wasn't any at the scene. I wasn't sure how Cassie had died, but it wasn't with a gun.

Then I followed up with a text to Penny asking her to look after my husband and feed him some chocolate if he started to look dizzy.

After a half hour wait, the chief joined me on the dock. "Well, shall we get down to it? You should know the routine by now, Mrs. McGhie."

He asked me the standard questions that I had come to expect each time I found a dead body in Coconut Cove. When he paused to jot something down in his notebook, I turned the tables and asked him a few questions.

"Who do you think killed her?"

"No comment."

"Do you think it's related to her husband's death?"

"No comment," he said, flipping to the next page in his notebook.

"One of the greeting cards on the table said that Cassie deserved to die, because of what she did. What do you think she did?"

He narrowed his eyes, then said, "No comment."

"How did she die?"

The chief was surprisingly loquacious when he answered this question. "That's for the coroner to determine." He snapped his notebook shut. "I think we're done here. I'll be in touch if I have any follow-up questions."

"What if I have any follow-up questions? What's the best way to get a hold of you? Phone or email? Should I come to the police station?"

Although he gave me a stern look, I could have sworn the sides of his mouth twitched as he suppressed a smile.

* * *

After I finished up with Chief Dalton, I caught up with Scooter, Ben, and Penny. The auditions had been canceled when Cassie had been discovered dead, so they had gone to the sports pavilion to collect Mrs. Moto.

The three of them were seated at a picnic table outside the building. Mrs. Moto was sprawled on top of the table, her fur covered in catnip, and a glazed look in her eyes.

"What happened to her box?" I asked.

"A poodle started chewing on it," Scooter said. "Needless to say, she wasn't too pleased."

"It is weird," I said. "She loves all other kinds of dogs, but, for some reason, she doesn't like poodles."

"Yeah, I know," Scooter said. "She didn't want anything to do with the box once the poodle had been near it, so we came out here instead and had a little catnip."

"Enough about poodles," Ben said. "Tell us what happened with Cassie. How did she die?"

"It looked like an overdose to me." I described the empty bottle of vodka and pills scattered on the floor.

"So, it was suicide," Penny said.

I shook my head. "My gut is telling me that someone else was involved. Cassie had been known to drink until she passed out, but no one had ever mentioned her taking pills."

Penny looked skeptical. "Maybe no one knew about the pills."

"Or maybe they weren't hers. Maybe she didn't even take any pills, and they were just left at the scene as a distraction. Maybe someone put poison in the vodka and then encouraged her to drink it or maybe ..."

My voice trailed off as I realized that I didn't have a clue how Cassie had died. All I knew was that someone had killed her, either directly or indirectly. I didn't have any proof that it was murder, but I knew with every fiber of my being that that was exactly what had happened.

Chief Dalton would have scoffed if I had told him about what my gut was telling me about Cassie's death. "A proper investigation is based on cold, hard evidence, Mrs. McGhie," he would have most likely said to me. "Stay out of police matters. Save your hunches for your UFOs and little green men."

He probably would have also added, "And stop asking me if I'm going to propose to Anabel."

I mentally shook myself. I needed to get the chief's negative thoughts out of my head and focus on proving my theory. After explaining to the others about the greeting cards I had found next to Cassie's body, I mused about what they meant.

"I think someone was trying to make a point about Cassie's drinking problem," I said. "The original trivia had been crossed out and replaced with alcohol-related ones. The person who did it was clever. They used crafting techniques so that it couldn't be traced back to them."

"Crafting techniques?" Ben asked.

"Stencils, stamps, that kind of thing," I explained.

"Oh, like how they used to do ransom notes in the old days by cutting out letters from newspapers?" Ben asked.

Scooter chuckled. "I'm surprised you know what old-fashioned print newspapers are considering what a youngster you are."

"I saw it in a movie once. I suppose that you're old enough to have had a paper route when you were a boy," Ben joked.

"I sure did," Scooter said.

"But you said that the last card—the one that said she deserved to die—had handwriting on it," Penny interjected.

"Yes, it had Cassie's name written on it. But I think Cassie wrote it herself."

"How do you know that?" Scooter asked.

"Do you remember the morning after the semi-finals when Mrs. Moto chased a lizard onto Cassie's boat, *Factoid*?" Scooter nodded. "Well, she ... ahem ... came back with an envelope." I gave the calico a pointed look, which she studiously ignored. "Cassie had written Trevor's name on it in the same fancy calligraphy."

"So, that just goes to prove that it was suicide," Penny said. "The card was her form of a suicide note."

"I'm not so sure about that." I pulled up the picture of the card on my phone. "See how it's written in third person —'Which television host deserves to die for what *she* did?' Cassie would have said something like, '*I* deserve to die, because of what *I* did.'"

"I suppose that's possible," Penny conceded.

I zoomed in on the bottom half of the card. "Look closely at the 'C' in Cassie's name. Do you see how it's partially covered by that sticker, the one that says 'did' at the end of the death threat? Somebody applied that sticker after Cassie wrote her name."

"Let me see that," Scooter said.

I handed him the phone, surprised that all this talk about death wasn't making him feel woozy. Maybe he was starting to get used to the surprisingly high murder rate in Coconut Cove.

"I think you're right," he said. "It looks like it was a set-up to make it seem like Cassie killed herself. Now all you have to do is prove it."

CHAPTER 14
OVERLY HAIRY TOES

Scooter's fortitude didn't last long. After telling me that I needed to prove that Cassie was murdered, he immediately retracted his statement and dug in my purse for chocolate. I gave him the last of my Reese's mini-peanut butter cups, then suggested that he take Mrs. Moto back to the boat while I did some errands. He wisely didn't ask what those errands were.

My first stop was the police station to see if I could find out when the coroner's preliminary report might be in. While I was convinced that Cassie had been murdered, it would be comforting to know that the coroner concurred with my assessment. Unfortunately, Charmaine Buttercup was on break and the police officer covering the front desk wasn't exactly forthcoming with information.

As I was heading back down Main Street, I spotted Kyle walking into the rose garden. I still had a lot of questions about Alejandra's mysterious ex-boyfriend, and now was the perfect opportunity to get them answered.

As I walked through the entrance, I saw him sitting on one of the benches staring at his phone. He startled when he saw me standing in front of him.

"Mind if I sit down?" I asked.

"Sure," he said, although he looked pointedly at the other empty benches.

"I don't know if you remember me. I'm one of Alejandra's friends."

He had the decency to look embarrassed when I mentioned her name. "Yeah, I think I've seen you around."

"What exactly happened with the two of you?"

For a moment, it looked like he wasn't going to answer. Then he sighed and said, "She's the type of girl I could seriously fall for. Pretty, smart, independent." He scrubbed his jaw. "But she deserves someone better than me."

"Well, I can't say that I disagree. You went to her parents' house for dinner, got in some sort of fight with her brother, and left without a word. Then dumped her."

"Yeah, I was a real jerk."

"The worst part is that she doesn't know why you broke up with her. You didn't even have the courage to do it face to face. You sent her a text."

"Trust me, it was better that way."

"No, it was probably easier that way ...

for you."

He stood before pacing back and forth for a few moments, nearly trampling over Mrs. McDougall's newly planted rose bushes in the process. Then he spun around, fixing me with a plaintive look. "How could I have told her the truth? What do you think her reaction would have been if I told her how I had an affair with a married woman?"

I raised my eyebrows. "A married woman? You were seeing someone else at the same time?"

"No, it was before I started dating Alejandra. And it really wasn't an affair as much as it was a one-night stand. Well, okay, a few-nights stand." He slumped back down on the bench and raked his fingers through his hair. "It was a mistake. A mistake that I regret. I tried to tell Miguel that, but he told me that he would never let his sister date a guy like me."

"Is that what you guys fought about

that night?"

"Yeah." Kyle put his head in his hands. "He saw a picture on my phone."

"Of you and the married woman? How did that happen?"

"Miguel and I were in the garage looking at a car he was working on. Cassie texted—"

"Whoa, wait a minute. You had an affair with Cassie Newton?"

"A few-nights stand," he clarified. "Anyway, she texted me, but I ended up dropping my phone. Miguel picked it up to hand it back to me, but when he saw the picture she sent—it was pretty racy —he freaked out. I tried to explain that it was ancient history, but he wouldn't listen. He told me that his sister had been two-timed before and that he didn't want to see her hurt again."

"Why didn't you just explain to Alejandra that it had taken place before she came into the picture and that Miguel had jumped to conclusions?"

"Miguel was right in a way. I wasn't seeing Cassie at the same time as Alejandra, but I did cheat on a girlfriend in the past." Kyle wrung his hands together. "Alejandra is a nice woman. She deserves someone better than me. I took the easy way out. I left without saying goodbye to her and sent her a text instead."

"The truth might have been hard for her to hear, but it would have given her some closure." He nodded, then I turned the conversation back to Cassie. "Did her husband know about the two of you?"

"Well, that's where things get complicated." He gave a brittle laugh. "Oh, what the heck, I might as well tell you the whole story. It'll feel good to get it off my chest, and it's not like it's ever going to work out with Alejandra, anyway. You see, I used to work for Robert."

"Doing what?"

"I'm a private investigator, or rather I *was* a private investigator." He grimaced. "I'm currently unemployed."

"Oh, my gosh, you're the guy that Anabel told me about the other day at the Sugar Shack."

"Who's Anabel?"

"She's the chief of police's ex-wife, although the 'ex' part is temporary. I'm pretty sure they're going to get remarried." I waved my hand in the air. "Anyway, that's not important."

"Okay," he said slowly. "What did this Anabel say about me?"

"She said that there was a private investigator in town and that the chief was irritated that he didn't have the courtesy to check in with him first."

Kyle furrowed his brow. "But I did come into the police station when I arrived in Coconut Cove. I told the receptionist who I was, but she said that the chief was too busy to see me."

"Was that Charmaine Buttercup?

Strawberry blonde hair? From Arkansas? Chatterbox?"

"No, her name was something like Judy or Janet. She had dark hair and didn't say much." He smiled. "I think I would have remembered someone named Charmaine Buttercup."

"I bet that was the former receptionist. She quit without notice and probably never told Chief Dalton that you stopped by." I shook my head. "Okay, let's get back to your story. You're a private investigator who worked for Robert Ronaldo."

"Correct. It all started with my great-uncle, Tony. He and Robert went way back. They were both in the Army together and when they got out, they both ended up in St. Louis. Whenever Robert needed someone to do his dirty work, he'd contact Tony."

"What kind of dirty work?"

"Oh, nothing illegal ... well, not all that illegal ... if that's what you're thinking.

When Robert hung up his gloves, he went into property development. One of the reasons he did so well is that Tony would dig up dirt on his competitors, then Robert would, let's see, how do I put this?"

"Blackmail them?" I suggested.

He shrugged. "You could call it that."

"So how did you get involved?"

"I went to work for Tony. His health isn't as good as it used to be, so he'd send me out into the field to look into things for Robert."

"Is that how you met Cassie?"

"Yes. Robert was holding a big charity ball and wanted me there to spy on this guy for him. Cassie was there and, well, one thing led to another." His face reddened. "It was a mistake. A huge mistake. Then a couple of months later when Robert called me and said that he suspected that Cassie was cheating on him and that he wanted me to find proof ... well, you can imagine what a jam I was in."

"So, what did you do?"

"What could I do? Tony had told him that I was in Coconut Cove working on another investigation for someone else. Since Cassie was in town for her show, Robert wanted me to tail her in my spare time."

"Oh, the fraud investigation. That's what you were working on."

He cocked his head to one side. "How did you know about that?"

"A buddy of the chief's told him about it—that's how he knew there was an investigator in town. He told Anabel, and she told me."

"It seems like it's hard to keep a secret in this town."

"What can I say? Small towns are like that. So what did you say to Robert when he asked you to investigate his wife?"

"I told him that I was too busy with the other investigation, which was true. He was furious. So furious that I was actually worried that he might do something to Cassie. I texted her and filled her in. Then I made the mistake of asking if she had any compromising photos of us. I didn't want them to come back on us. That's when she sent me the one that Miguel saw."

"Okay. That all makes sense so far, but there are a few things I don't understand. First, I saw you at the Tipsy Pirate the night of the semi-finals. You were having a heated discussion with Cassie. She gave you an envelope stuffed with cash."

"You saw that?"

"Everyone saw that," I said. "What I want to know is what the cash was for. Was it a payoff?"

He folded his arms across his chest. "I may have done a lot of things I'm ashamed of, but I have never taken a payoff. If you really saw what happened, then you'll know that I didn't take the envelope. She shoved it in my pocket."

"That's true, I saw that part. I also heard you say as much to Cassie later at her boat. But she tried to pay you off for something, didn't she?"

He nodded. "Cassie wanted me to lie to Robert. She had called me earlier that evening and pleaded with me to tell Robert that I had done a thorough investigation of her. To tell him that I was convinced that she was one hundred percent faithful to him. She was worried about her prenup. She would have lost a fortune if Robert could have proven that she cheated on him."

"But she must have had her own money from being on TV," I said.

"She did make good money, but Robert made more. A lot more." He shook his head. "What she couldn't get through her thick head was that, sooner or later, Robert was going to get proof of her adultery. I wasn't the first guy she had an affair with, and I wouldn't have been the last."

I chewed on my lip for a moment, recalling the night of the semi-finals when Cassie had threatened someone on the phone. A threat that everyone at the Tipsy Pirate had heard. "You mentioned that Cassie had phoned you. Did she say something like, 'Over your dead body'?"

"That sounds about right. Cassie could be very dramatic when she had a few drinks in her. That's why I came by the bar, to talk with her in person about it." He took a deep breath, then exhaled. "When Alejandra came up to me, I panicked. I was worried that Miguel had told her about the photo he saw on my phone so I—"

"Acted like a jerk to her, giving her a cold shoulder."

He stared down at the ground, his jaw tight. Then he cleared his throat. "Like I said, I've done a lot of things I'm not proud of. How I treated Alejandra is one of them."

"Are you up for a few more questions?"

"Shoot."

"The money in the envelope wasn't American, was it?"

He looked back up at me. "Uh, no. How did you know that?"

"I saw you at the waterfront park looking at it. Where was the cash from?"

"A Caribbean country. I know that Robert was doing a deal there. It was all a little dodgy from what I understand. I'm not sure how Cassie got her hands on the money. Maybe took it from their safe. Although, how she thought Robert wouldn't notice that is beyond me. It's hard to believe that she has a graduate degree given some of the stupid things she's done."

"Okay, so that's answered that question."

"You have more?"

"Uh-huh." I looked around the rose

garden. While normally I appreciated how quiet and peaceful it was, right now I was grateful for the couple who had just walked in, because my next question was a bit dangerous. "So, did you kill Robert?"

Kyle's eyes grew wide, then he broke into laughter. "That's your question? Did I kill Robert?"

"Well, did you?" I prompted. "You were probably worried that he'd find out about you and Cassie."

"No," he said, once he managed to stop laughing. "I was out of town when the murder happened. And, yes, before you ask, I can prove it."

Which he proceeded to do, pulling up an article online showing him at a baseball game in St. Louis, his arm around a young kid who was grinning ear-to-ear. "I'm part of a community mentoring program. We had an event the night Robert was killed."

"Okay," I said, relieved that Kyle had

an alibi. Sure, he was a jerk for how he treated Alejandra, not to mention his dalliance with a married woman, but at least he wasn't a killer. The last thing my friend needed was to think that she had dated a murderer.

"So who do you think did it? Cassie? When you came to her boat to return the money, she said that she wouldn't have done what she did if you hadn't agreed to take the money." Kyle held up his hand in protest. "I know you didn't take it, she shoved it in your pocket, but what I'm interested in is what she meant by what she said. What did she do? Did she kill her husband? Chief Dalton said that she had an iron-clad alibi for that night, but maybe he was wrong."

"Hmm ... you overheard that conversation as well. Wow, you do seem to know everything." He smiled faintly. "You'd make a good private investigator."

"I'm not so sure about that. It seems

like lately, all I have to go on is what my gut tells me, but I don't have any facts to back it up."

"Don't underestimate the importance of trusting your gut. Your intuition is a good starting point. But if you want some facts, I have a few for you. First, Cassie filed for divorce. She assumed that I'd cover up her affairs so that it would go through without a problem. Second, Cassie did have an alibi for the night Robert was killed. I know that for a fact. When I didn't agree to investigate her, Robert hired a buddy of mine. He saw her that night sitting on the deck of her boat, passed out."

"At the exact time when Robert was killed?"

"Uh-huh."

"But then why did she try to bribe people to say that they had seen Alejandra's brother kill Robert?"

"She wouldn't have known that someone had been watching her. And since she didn't have an alibi, she would have been worried that they would have tried to pin the blame for Robert's death on her. In her twisted mind, it was easier to get people to lie for her then tell the truth."

"Okay, that makes sense," I said. "I just have a few more questions."

Kyle looked at his phone. "I have a plane to catch, so we'll have to keep it short."

"When I saw you at the waterfront park, you were on the phone. You said something about showing someone proof, but that he didn't pay you. What was that about?"

"That had to do with the fraud investigation I was working on. The client had me do the job, then didn't want to pay me. Not all clients are easy to deal with."

"So who is committing fraud in Coconut Cove?" I asked, my curiosity piqued.

"Sorry, I can't say. But what I can tell you is that it's completely unrelated to Robert." He tapped his phone. "I need to get going."

"All right, final question. You also said something on the phone about keeping the cash Cassie had given you. What was that about?"

"No, what I said was, 'You think I should keep the cash?'" He frowned. "My uncle tried to convince me that I should. That's one of the reasons why I quit working for him. It wouldn't have been the right thing to do. I need to get out of this game before I turn into someone that I don't want to be."

He stood and shoved his phone in his pocket. "I'll tell you what, since you're hot on investigating Robert and Cassie's murders, I've got something you might want to look into. Robert Ronaldo wasn't always Robert Ronaldo."

"Huh? What does that mean?"

"He changed his name before he got

into property development. Try googling the name 'George Jones' and see what comes up." As he walked toward the gate, he said over his shoulder, "Please tell Alejandra that I'm sorry."

* * *

Do you know what happens when you google "George Jones"? You find out a lot about country music, but very little about murders in Coconut Cove. I spent a couple of hours trying to make the connection with Robert Ronaldo, but eventually had to put that task to the side while Scooter and I worked on boat projects.

The next afternoon, after we had finished installing a new stove, I decided to head to the Seaside Center instead to see if any of the tenants could shed any light on the matter.

When I walked through the entrance to the Nail Nook, my jaw dropped. Chief

Dalton was sitting in one of the spa chairs, the bottoms of his pants rolled up, and his feet submerged in water. Alejandra was perched on a stool in front of him, applying moisturizer to his calves.

"Are you getting a pedicure?" I asked with a smirk.

The chief startled, almost dropping the cup of tea in his hand. "Uh ... Mrs. McGhie ... what are you doing here?"

Alejandra smiled at me. "Anabel got him a gift certificate. Wasn't that sweet of her?"

"It sure was," I said, sitting in the chair next to the chief. "Maybe I should get one for Scooter. But I have to say that I'm surprised that you're here having your toes done when there's a killer on the loose."

The burly man set his cup down and glared at me. "We're waiting for the coroner's report, my officers are busy investigating leads, and I'm here—"

"Getting your cuticles done?"

As he continued to glare at me, I realized that the chief was too responsible to be getting a pedicure in the midst of an investigation. That meant only one thing—he was there undercover.

I leaned over and whispered, "Don't worry, I won't blow your cover."

"My cover?"

"Shush," I said. "Keep your voice down. You don't want everyone to hear you. Just act normal and I'll do the talking. There's something I think you should look into—the chocolate box."

"What chocolate box?"

"You know what box I'm talking about. The one that was in Robert's briefcase."

"No comment."

I shrugged. "Fine, you don't have to comment. You just have to listen. I saw the box on Cassie's boat. The interesting thing about it is that it had a new logo that Angus had designed. But there were only two people who supposedly got boxes with that logo— me and another guy who was in the chocolate shop the day after Robert was killed. If that's the case, how did Robert get a hold of that box the day before? Did Angus leave it at the scene when he killed him?"

Before he could respond with another 'no comment,' the door to the nail salon flew open. Francine stood at the entrance, her hands on her hips. "Where's my paycheck? You still owe me for the time I worked here."

Alejandra frowned. "Excuse me for a moment." She rose from her stool and wiped her hands with a towel.

Francine strode toward us. "It didn't come in the mail today."

"That's because it was direct deposited," Alejandra said calmly.

"That's not true. I didn't deposit it."

"No, I know you didn't deposit it. It was automatically deposited into your account."

"Automatic? What are you talking about?"

Alejandra sighed. "You filled out the direct deposit paperwork when I hired you. Why don't you look up your account on your phone? You'll see that your money was deposited today."

Francine shook her head, her silver curls bouncing. "I do my banking the old-fashioned way, by going into the bank, not by looking on a phone. But I suppose that's not how you young people do it these days, is it?"

"Why don't you come up front with me and we can look it up on the computer."

While Francine continued to argue with Alejandra at the reception area, I slid off my chair and sat on Alejandra's stool.

"What are you doing, Mrs. McGhie?" the chief asked.

"We have to keep up your cover. I'll pretend to be your nail technician. Now, let's see, where was Alejandra? Oh, yeah, giving you a calf massage." I picked up the bottle of lotion and squeezed some onto my hands. "Ooh, that smells like lemon verbena."

The chief pulled his feet out of the tub. "You're not going to give me a pedicure. I knew this was a bad idea. I told Anabel that my feet look fine the way they are."

"Um, I'm not so sure about that." I grimaced. "I don't think I've ever seen such hairy toes. Have you ever thought about waxing them?"

The chief spluttered, "Uh … Wax?"

Then we both turned to look at Francine slamming Alejandra's laptop shut. "All I want is a regular, normal paper check. And I need it now. I promised my daughter that I'd make dinner tonight since she's working and I need to get to the store to pick up some lima beans."

Alejandra held her hands up and made soothing noises. "I'll tell you what, why don't we both go down to the bank together and see what we can do."

"Lima beans," I muttered to myself, absentmindedly rubbing lotion onto the chief's feet.

"What are you doing, Mrs. McGhie?"

I looked down, then recoiled at the fact that I had just touched his hairy toes. Quickly rubbing my hands with a towel, I jumped back into the seat next to him.

"Francine mentioned lima beans," I said in an undertone. "Do you know what dish you put lima beans in? Succotash."

The chief rolled his eyes. "A minute ago, you were talking about pedicures, now you're talking about cooking."

"No, hear me out. The other day when I was talking to Francine, her grandson told me about a boxer named 'Hoppin' Succotash.' At least that's what I thought he was saying. But now I'm not so sure. I think he might have been saying 'Jumping Sassafras.' He's missing his front teeth." I pulled my phone out of my purse and did a quick search. "Oh, my gosh, here it is. Jumping Sassafras was a boxer in St. Louis whose real name was, wait for it, George Jones."

"You've lost me."

"Robert Ronaldo used to be George Jones. This picture of him dressed as a boxer is the same one I saw on Cassie's boat. I thought he had been dressed up for a costume party, but he wasn't. He really was a boxer."

"Still lost."

"Listen, the night that Robert Ronaldo was murdered, he was standing right outside the nail salon. When Francine saw him, she said 'Jumping Sassafras.' When I asked her about it, she passed it off as an old expression of her grandmother's, but what I think really happened is that she recognized Robert Ronaldo back from when she was his manicurist in St. Louis."

The chief took a sip of his tea. "Go on."

"And here's where it gets interesting. Francine told me that she had an affair with a guy. He had fathered her child, but wouldn't acknowledge her. Then he disappeared off the face of the earth. What if, after all these years, Francine finally saw him again? She was angry, really angry about him abandoning her and their daughter. What if she decided to confront him that night? He probably scoffed and denied knowing her. That would have enraged her. Then, one thing led to another, and she took her revenge, shooting him with his own gun."

The chief set down his cup. "Do you see my shoes around here anywhere?"

"Are you going to speak with Francine? You better hurry. She and Alejandra just left to go to the bank." The burly man ignored me while he unrolled his pants and tied his shoes. As he got up to leave, I added, "Don't forget to come back and get your pedicure finished. If you and Anabel decide to get married on the beach, you'll want your feet looking their best."

CHAPTER 15
CLOWNS ON ROLLER COASTERS

Exhausted from trying to get Chief Dalton back on track with the investigation, I headed back to the marina. As I walked down the dock, I saw Brittany sitting on the deck of Cassie's boat. She waved when she saw me.

"How did *Factoid* get here?" I asked, surprised to see it back in the slip opposite from my sailboat.

"I brought it back," she said. "Once the

police had finished with it, they needed it moved from the public docks and I offered to help."

"That was nice of you."

"It was no big deal. I need to get some stuff off it that belongs to the production company, anyway. Besides, it was nice to be back on the water again."

"Brittany, where did you put my shirt?" a voice yelled up from below. "You know, the one I got for my birthday."

"Hang on a minute," she said to me, then poked her head into the pilothouse. "It's on the table."

"Sorry about that." She clapped her hands together. "Did you hear the good news? I'm going to be the new host of *Triviamania*."

"Congratulations. I guess there was a silver lining to Cassie's death."

"And I have some more good news," she said, ignoring my pointed comment about Cassie. "We're going to reschedule the auditions for next month.

You should wear that cute pom-pom outfit again."

Before I could explain that my qutrit costume had been turned into a cat toy, Trevor walked out on deck. "Brittany, I still can't find my shirt. Last time I saw it you had it while I was pouring all of those bottles of booze out."

"Ahem, we have company," she said.

Trevor looked over at me sharply. "Oh, sorry, I didn't see you there. It's Mollie, right? You were at the Hazelton Estate with your husband the other day, meeting with Cassie about the auditions."

"I already told her about the auditions being rescheduled," Brittany said brightly. "And about how I was here on the boat to get stuff off it that belonged to the production company." She looked at me. "Trevor's helping with that."

I furrowed my brow. "Is that what people in public relations normally do?"

Brittany cocked her head to one side.

"Public relations?"

Trevor placed his hand on her arm. "Yes, don't you remember? Cassie hired me to work for her."

"Oh, sure," Brittany said quickly. "I'm just used to hearing people call it PR rather than public relations. Anyway, we should probably get a move on. This boat isn't going to sort itself out."

After saying a hasty goodbye to me, the two of them walked into the pilothouse. The problem with having curtains up is that sometimes you don't realize that the windows are open, which is why I heard Brittany hiss at Trevor. "We really need to get our stories straight."

I rolled my eyes. Trevor had no idea that I had seen him previously in a passionate embrace with Cassie. I already knew the real story about the two of them and their affair.

* * *

The next morning, Scooter and I were in the cockpit of our boat, sipping on coffee and waiting for Ben to arrive. While Ben was helping Scooter climb up the mast so that he could check on our anchor light, I had plans to meet Charmaine Buttercup at the Sailor's Corner Cafe for breakfast.

She had phoned me earlier to give me the scoop on Cassie's death. While it wasn't official—it would take a while to get all the tests back—the coroner believed that she had died as a result of alcohol poisoning combined with a drug overdose. She could have killed herself, but there were suspicious bruises on Cassie's arms, shoulders, and jaw, almost as though someone had forced the alcohol and pills down her throat, leading him to suspect foul play. Charmaine promised to give me more details when we met up.

Having breakfast plans, however, didn't stop me from enjoying a freshly baked chocolate croissant. I considered it a pre-breakfast. Something to give me enough energy to drive to the cafe.

"Penelope sure is winning with these bake-at-home pastries." I licked chocolate off my fingers. When Scooter didn't respond, I glanced over at him. He was frowning as he typed something on his phone. "What's wrong?"

"Ben can't help today. Something about having to work an extra shift at the marina office. Ned and Nancy were supposed to be back last night from their vacation, but their flight got canceled."

"Maybe he can help out tomorrow."

Scooter raised his eyebrows. "Have you seen the forecast? There's a system forming off the coast. We're going to get pretty hammered here over the next few days. No, it will have to wait until Ben has some free time next week."

I chewed on my lip for a moment. Scooter had been wanting to tick this project off our "Set Sail to the Bahamas" to do list. Boat projects had been frustrating him lately, and he had been bummed when he had to cancel going up the mast with Ben the previous week due to his stomach bug.

"Fine I'll do it," I said. "I'll go up the mast."

"Don't be silly. Ben and I can take care of it some other time."

"No, really, I want to help. I heard a lady talking about it on the patio the other day. She was saying that when they sailed to Fiji, something happened to their rigging and one of them had to go up. He's a big guy and she's a tiny woman. There was no way that she could have hoisted him up, so she volunteered to go aloft."

"But that's why I have Ben helping," Scooter said. "He's strong and can hoist me up."

"Sure, that's fine here at the marina. But what if something happens out there? I have to be able to go up there in an emergency. My first time might as well be here where it's safe."

Scooter shook his head. "You don't have to do this, Mollie."

I smiled when he called me by my first name instead of one of his silly pet names. Generally, it meant that he knew he was going to be in trouble—like the time the ants had escaped from their ant farms and discovered a jar of peanut butter Scooter had left open in the kitchen. Though there were other times when he called me Mollie, usually when he was worried about me.

"Seriously," he continued. "I know that you've been scared of heights ever since what happened at—"

"Please don't talk about that." I shuddered. "Roller coasters and clowns. I should have known that would be a bad idea."

"Really, Mollie. You don't have to."

"Are there going to be any clowns involved?"

Scooter smiled and shook his head.

"And no sudden ups and downs like a roller coaster, right?"

"No. I'll make sure you go up and down nice and easy."

"Okay then, let's get this show on the road before I change my mind."

After calling Charmaine and asking if we could meet for lunch instead, Scooter helped me get into the bosun's chair. I sat on what was essentially a padded plank, slipping my legs around either side of a crotch strap. He adjusted the waist strap, then asked me if I was comfortable.

"So far, so good," I said.

"Sitting in a bosun's chair can get uncomfortable after a while—your legs might go numb and your butt might get sore."

"Way to sell it."

"Don't worry, we'll have you down before that happens." He gave me a peck on the cheek, then fastened a line to the bosun's chair. "This is the halyard for our mainsail. Instead of using it to hoist the sail, I'll use it to hoist you in the air."

I looked up at the top of our mast and gulped. "Talk me through how that's going to work again."

"I'll wrap the halyard around the winch, just like we do with the sail, put the handle in the winch and crank you up. When you get to the top, I'll tie the line off securely on the cleat."

"Emphasis on 'securely', okay?"

"Don't worry. If something should happen to that line, you'll have a secondary safety line as back-up."

"You're using our spinnaker halyard for that safety line, right?"

He grinned. "Look at how far you've come since we got *Marjorie Jane* for our tenth wedding anniversary. A year ago, you wouldn't have had a clue what a halyard or a spinnaker were. You would have described a halyard as a rope that pulls stuff up and you would have said that a spinnaker is a really big, colorful sail."

"Which is accurate, I should point out."

"True, but now you sound like a sailor." He tugged at the mainsail halyard. "I'm going to hoist you up just a foot or so. You'll dangle in the chair. I want you to bounce up and down as hard as you can so that we can make sure everything is secure."

After performing our safety checks, Scooter gave me one more opportunity to back out. "Nope, no way, mister. I'm already in this contraption. Let's get it over with."

I managed to get to the halfway point without freaking out, primarily by distracting myself by singing Elvis tunes. When you're trying to remember the lyrics to *Jailhouse Rock*, you tend to forget how high up you are in the air.

Then the boat started rocking from side-to-side violently. I had been holding onto the mast as Scooter slowly hoisted me up, but I lost my grip, causing me to swing back and forth like Tarzan in search of a vine to grab hold of. After what seemed like an eternity, I finally got hold of the mast again, bruising both my knees in the process.

"Are you okay, Mollie?" Scooter called out. "That was wake from some jerk in his powerboat speeding through the marina."

"I'm fine," I said. "Let's keep going before he wakes us again."

Once I neared the top of the mast, Scooter tied off both lines securely. "Okay, I'm going to go back to the stern of the boat and keep an eye on you from there. That way if you accidentally drop one of your tools, it won't clobber me in the head. If you need anything, just yell. Okay?"

After assuring him that I was fine, I got to work inspecting the anchor light. I pulled a screwdriver out of the tool bag attached to the bosun's chair and wrapped my other hand around the mast to secure me. Instead of feeling the smooth metal of the mast that I expected, I touched something that had an odd, bumpy dirt-like texture.

That's when the buzzing started.

Wondering what the heck could be on the other side of the mast that made a buzzing noise, I pulled myself around to get a better view.

The buzzing got louder and it sounded angry. Which was strange as inanimate objects, like masts, don't generally get angry. Toasters do sometimes, but that's a whole other story.

Then I saw what was making that insistent, angry buzzing noise.

Wasps. Lots and lots of wasps.

Wasps that were far from happy that I

had disturbed their hive.

They swarmed toward me, and I screamed. I dropped the screwdriver. Then I screamed again.

"Mollie, what's going on?" Scooter yelled.

Before I could answer, the boat started rocking back and forth again, and I swung side-to-side, batting wildly at the wasps.

"Scooter, get me down from here!" When he didn't answer, I yelled again for him to lower me to the deck. "Scooter, answer me, please. Get me down! Hurry!"

Then I screamed again, but not because of attacking wasps. No, this time I screamed because I was plummeting to my death.

* * *

The emergency room doctor reviewed Scooter's chart, then examined the back of his head. "The good news is that you don't need stitches."

"No stitches? But there's bl ... bl ..." Scooter swallowed, then looked at me.

"I think what my husband is trying to say is that there's a lot of ..." I put my hand to the side of my face so that Scooter couldn't see what I was saying, then whispered, "blood everywhere."

The doctor gave me a funny look, then said, "He has a head injury. They bleed a lot, but it generally looks worse than it really is."

Scooter clutched his stomach and groaned. The doctor rushed over. "Are you having abdominal pains, sir? When you were admitted, you said that you had been hit over the head with a winch handle. Do you remember being hit anywhere else? Any other injuries we don't know about?"

Scooter shook his head, then reached out and squeezed my hand.

"It was just a reaction to you saying

the 'B' word," I said.

"The 'B' word?" The doctor's eyes grew wide. "Goodness, no … I never said that. I would never say anything like that."

I cocked my head to one side, then realization dawned on me. "No, not *that* 'B' word. The other 'B' word."

After asking the doctor to come out into the hallway, I explained to him that Scooter couldn't cope with anyone mentioning blood, let alone seeing it. I suggested that he use a code word instead, something like 'ketchup' or 'strawberry jam.' He offered to give me a referral to a therapist. I wasn't entirely sure if it was for me or Scooter, but before I could clarify, Chief Dalton arrived.

"How's Mr. McGhie?" he asked. "Is he up for some questions?"

"Physically, he's fine. We do want to keep him here for a while to make sure he doesn't have a concussion," the doctor said. "However, he was a little spooked by all the ... uh ... tomato sauce"

The chief gave me a sideways look. "He means blood, doesn't he?"

"You know how Scooter gets."

"Yeah. Good thing he didn't go into medicine or police work," the chief said.

The doctor excused himself, saying he'd be back later to check on the patient. After he left, the chief turned to me, a surprisingly gentle tone to his voice. "And how are you? I heard you had quite a scare."

"I was lucky that the safety line got caught on the radar dome and saved me from crashing into the deck." I ran my fingers through my hair. "I still can't believe someone smacked Scooter over the head, then undid both of the lines attached to my bosun's chair."

"And you don't know who it was?"

"No, like I told the officer at the scene, all I saw was someone at the bottom of the mast wearing some sort of top with a hood. I couldn't see their face. You have to remember that I was almost sixty feet in the air, being attacked by wasps."

"You realize that they were mud daubers, right? They usually don't attack humans, unlike other types of wasps." The chief wrote something down in his notebook, then glanced at me. "And Mr. McGhie doesn't remember anything?"

"No, he was hit from behind. He didn't notice anyone come on board, because the boat was already rocking back and forth. Some jerk speeding in a powerboat. You guys should do something about that. You have speed traps for cars, why not for boats?"

The chief's suppressed a smile. "Not really my department, but I'll make a note of that." Then his expression grew more seriously. "We need to talk about who might have done this."

"It has to do with the murders. The killer must have thought I knew who him ... or her is. But I don't have a clue." I paced back and forth in the hallway, trying to process my thoughts. "Originally, I thought there were five people who could have killed Robert— Cassie, Francine, Angus, Brittany, or Trevor. Cassie had an alibi. That private investigator saw her on the deck of her boat the night her husband was killed, so that ruled her out. Then, I thought Trevor might have done it on Cassie's behalf, but he had an alibi too. He had been with a buddy at the Tipsy Pirate that night. One of Ben's buddies was there. That left me with Francine, Angus, and Brittany."

I paused, stepping aside to let a nurse pushing a gurney get past me. Then I continued pacing. "Let's see, Brittany was the last person to be seen with Robert, but she didn't have any reason to kill him that I know of. That left

Francine and Angus. Both of them could have done it, and they both had a motive. Francine because Robert hadn't acknowledged that he was the father of her child, and Angus because his lease was being terminated."

"Mrs. McGhie, you're making me dizzy walking back and forth like that. Come sit down." He pointed at a row of plastic lime green chairs lining the wall.

I sat down next to him and sighed. "Where was I?"

"You were talking about the individuals who claimed they saw Mr. Lopez shoot Mr. Ronaldo. I actually have some information on them."

"You do?"

"After my ... um ..." The burly man cleared his throat, then lowered his voice, "pedicure, I looked into what you said about the chocolate box."

"Really? What did you find out?"

"When I spoke with Mr. Tanaka, he admitted that he had left a message for

Mr. Ronaldo asking him to come down to his shop the night of the murder."

"Oh, so it had been Angus," I said. "All the tenants had denied being the one who had called him."

"Well, he's admitted it now. He said that he begged Mr. Ronaldo not to terminate his lease. He even gave him a box of truffles to try. But Mr. Ronaldo told him that he hated chocolate, then stuffed them into his briefcase."

"So, that's how they ended up in there. I suppose Angus didn't want to admit that he had given the chocolate to Robert."

"No," the chief said. "That's why he said that you and that other man who was in his shop the next day were the first people to get boxes with the new cat logo on them."

"Okay, but he still could have killed Robert. Or Francine. She could have too. Neither of them had alibis for that night."

"That's true, but they both had alibis for when Cassie was killed."

I raised my eyebrows. "They do? When did that happen?"

"During the course of the investigation," the chief said.

"You could have shared that information with me," I said.

"No, it was on a need to know basis," he said.

I clenched my fists. "Someone just tried to kill me and they almost killed Scooter. I think I need to know now."

"I do too, which is why I'm sharing this information with you." The chief flipped through his notebook. "We know that Miss Murphy was with her daughter and grandson during the time that the coroner believes Cassie was killed—"

"Miss Murphy? Who is that?"

"Francine Murphy."

I shrugged. "I guess I never knew her last name. It might help if you were less formal and called people by their first names."

"That wouldn't be very professional of me, Mrs. McGhie." He tapped his notebook. "Like I was saying, Miss Murphy has an alibi. Mr. Tanaka ... Angus Tanaka—"

"I know Angus' last name."

"Fine. He was here at the hospital visiting a family member when Cassie Newton was killed."

"Okay, so Francine or Angus could have killed Robert, but they couldn't have killed Cassie." I put my head in my hands. "Why is this so complicated?"

"It's not complicated. It just requires a logical, methodical approach."

"Fine, let's be logical and methodical then. Who could have killed both Robert and Cassie?"

"No one."

"No one?"

"Mr. Wallace ..." the chief paused and glanced at me.

"Wait, I know this one ... Trevor

Wallace, the caretaker at the Hazelton Estate."

"Correct. He has an alibi for Mr. Ronaldo's murder, but he doesn't have one for Miss Newton's."

"Well, it's not like he would have killed Cassie," I said. "She had just hired him as her public relations consultant."

"And the other person on your list, Miss Abernethy, has an alibi for Miss Newton's murder, but not for Mrs. Ronaldo's."

"What was her alibi for when Cassie was killed?"

"She was getting things ready for the *Triviamania* auditions. The entire production team can vouch for her."

"So that rules out Francine, Angus, Trevor, and Brittany," I said, ticking their names off on my fingers. "Which leaves us with no one who could have killed both of them. That means that either the murders were unrelated, which seems unlikely or—"

Scooter stuck his head out into the hall. "There you are, my little qutrit. I'm thirsty. Do you think you could get me something to drink?"

"Sure. What do you want? Water, soda, juice?"

"Any chance you could find some lemonade for me? For some reason, I'm having a real craving for it. You don't think it could be a side effect of my head injury?"

I chuckled. "I doubt it. Go lie back down, and I'll see if I can find some for you."

As I started to push myself off the plastic chair, I noticed its lime green color. "Lemonade," I muttered. "... Lime green lemonade."

"What's that, Mrs. McGhie?" the chief asked.

"Oh, my goodness. I think I know who did it. Or, more accurately, who *plural* did it."

CHAPTER 16
ELVIS IS IN THE BUILDING

"It was Brittany and Trevor." I shifted on the plastic chair and fixed my gaze on the chief. "That's Miss Abernethy and Mr. Wallace to you. Brittany killed Robert and Trevor killed Cassie."

"How did you arrive at that conclusion?" Chief Dalton asked.

"By taking a logical and methodical approach." I grabbed my phone out of my purse. "Also this."

I pulled up the obituary for Brittany's parents that I had found earlier when I was looking into her background. "See how it says Mr. and Mrs. Abernethy left behind two children—a daughter, that's Brittany, and a son, that's Trevor."

"But it doesn't say Trevor. It says the son's name is Michael."

"Don't believe everything you read. He's using a fake name now. Happens all the time."

"But why would they have killed them?"

I grabbed my phone, pulled up an article from a Chicago newspaper, then handed it back to him. "Their parents were killed in a tragic car accident. It was a hit and run. A witness had originally come forward and said he saw the whole thing. He saw the driver of the other car come out of a bar, get into his car, and plow into the Abernethys' vehicle. But then he changed his story. Sound familiar?"

The chief pursed his lips. "Are you saying someone paid him off to change his story?"

"Bingo. Just like Cassie tried to do with Angus and Francine. I bet you anything that she bribed the eyewitness to change his story."

"But why would she do that?"

"If the truth had come out, it would have ruined Robert's career. Cassie liked being the wife of a wealthy man."

"Okay, that might be true," the chief said. "But how do you know that Trevor is really Michael Abernethy?"

"Brittany told Ben that she couldn't go out with him, because she needed to meet up with her brother. That was a slip on her part. She didn't want anyone to know that Trevor was her brother, let alone that he was in town. It would have messed up their plan."

"Their plan?"

"Retribution, vengeance, whatever you want to call it. They wanted Robert to pay for killing their parents, and they wanted Cassie to pay for covering it up.

Remember how when I told Brittany about Francine and Angus covering for Cassie, she told me that it wasn't the first time that Cassie had tried to pay someone off. She knew from personal experience that Cassie wasn't above that sort of thing."

He nodded slowly. "Assuming you're right, that Brittany and Trevor are brother and sister, and that they wanted to kill Robert and Cassie as a sort of revenge, you'll have to explain their plan, because it isn't very clear to me."

"Notice how you just called everyone by their first names? It's a lot easier, don't you think?"

He scowled, so I quickly continued. "I'm not sure they planned things out that precisely. What they did was get into a position where they could take their revenge when the time came. Brittany got a job working for *Triviamania*, and then she introduced her brother to Cassie."

I tapped my finger on my lips as I recalled my encounter with Brittany and Trevor the previous day at the marina. Trevor mentioned that Cassie had hired him to do public relations work. Brittany looked confused by that, but had quickly recovered. After they had said goodbye to me, I heard Brittany reprimanding him about not having their cover story straight.

After sharing that tidbit with the chief, I said, "Brittany knew that Cassie had a thing for younger guys who are easy on the eyes, so that helped seal the deal, so to speak. Then they just took advantage of opportunities as they presented themselves."

"So you're saying it wasn't pre-meditated?"

"I don't think Robert's murder was. I think Brittany really did come to the Seaside Center the night of Alejandra's grand opening to make an appointment for a manicure. Then, when she saw the tenants ganging up on Robert, she defused the situation and walked him to his car, which was parked in the overflow lot by the beach. Then, somehow, she got a hold of his gun."

The chief shot me a glance. I held my hands up. "Listen, I don't know how or why. Did he open his briefcase to get something out and she grabbed it? Did he realize who she really was, pulled the gun out to protect himself and she grabbed it then? That's the kind of thing you'll need to look into."

"So no hard evidence," the chief said dryly.

"No, just good solid investigative intuition," I retorted. "Anyway, moving on to Cassie's murder, there may have been some more planning there. I'll bet you anything that Trevor helped move her boat from the Palm Tree Marina to the public docks at the waterfront park. He and Brittany know all about boats, you know. Their parents had a sailboat and the two of them grew up sailing on Lake Michigan."

"So why do you think there was planning involved?"

"Two things. The greeting cards had been doctored. The original trivia facts had been crossed out and replaced with alcohol-related ones, obviously a reference to their parents being killed by a drunk driver. And remember the final card, the one that said Cassie Newton deserved to die for what she had done? Well, that was a reference to her covering up the fact that Robert had killed the Abernethys."

"So you think they altered the cards."

"Cassie had all of her card-making supplies at the Hazelton Estate. It would have been easy enough for him to have done it. He also just had a birthday. I heard him talk about a shirt he had gotten for his birthday with Brittany. Mrs. Moto also found an envelope with Trevor's name written on it in calligraphy. I bet you anything there had been a birthday card in it. One that Cassie had given him which she signed her name on with her special lilac ink. That's the one they used too."

"You mentioned two things. What was the other one?"

"The pills," I said. "They had to have gotten them from somewhere. Trevor knew that Cassie drank to excess. He probably cajoled her into having some of his 'special' cocktails, then forced enough pills down her throat to kill her."

"Special cocktails?"

"Oh, yeah." I scrolled through my photos until I came to the one I had taken aboard Factoid when I discovered that Cassie had been killed. "See that plastic bottle next to the pills on the floor? There's some green juice inside."

"Yes, I know. We had it tested. It was harmless. A mix of lemonade and—"

"Kiwi fruit," I interjected. "Cassie told me that it was a special blend that

Trevor made. It was very sweet. I bet she gulped it down."

The chief drummed his fingers on his notebook. "That makes sense. The alcohol in the bottle you saw wasn't vodka. It was one hundred ninety proof grain alcohol. The juice blend would have easily disguised that."

"One hundred ninety proof? I didn't think that was legal in Florida."

"It isn't."

"Let me guess. It's legal in Chicago where Trevor is from."

"Correct." The chief gave me an appraising look. "How did you make the connection to Trevor?"

"Remember when Scooter asked for lemonade?" After the chief nodded, I pointed at the seats we were sitting on. "See this lime-green color? It looks like the color of a kiwi fruit. I just put two and two together."

The burly man removed his cap and scratched his head. "Two and two," he muttered. Then he looked back at me. "Okay, assuming that what you've said is true, do you think one of them tried to kill you?"

"Yes. Like I said, they both grew up sailing. They would know what's involved in going up a mast and how dangerous it was. It would have been simple for one of them to put Scooter out of commission, then untie the lines."

"But how would they have known that you were going to go up the mast at that particular moment?"

"Good question." I chewed on my lip for a moment. "The only person who knew was Charmaine."

"Charmaine Buttercup? The police receptionist?"

"Do you know any other Charmaine Buttercups?" I held up my hand before he could say something snippy. "I was supposed to meet her for breakfast, but then Ben canceled. I agreed to go up the mast and called her to reschedule for lunch."

The chief grabbed his phone out of his pocket and quickly called the police station. After a brusque conversation, he turned back to me. "Trevor was there earlier complaining about a speeding ticket. He overheard Charmaine's call with you."

"Brittany was probably on board *Factoid* at the time. She's docked right across from our boat."

"He probably called his sister to let her know."

I sank back into my chair. "It was the perfect opportunity to get rid of me. They probably thought I had figured it all out."

The chief barked a few more orders on the phone, hung up, then turned back to me. "Your intuition paid off. It looks like you might have solved this one, Mrs. McGhie."

* * *

"Can I have everyone's attention, please?" Scooter stood at the head of the table, holding a thick envelope in his hand. "I have some news that I think you all will be very interested in hearing."

It was a few days after Brittany Abernethy and her brother, Trevor, also known as Michael, had been arrested for the murders of Robert Ronaldo and Cassie Newton. Trevor had caved first, confessing to killing Cassie. Brittany held out longer, but eventually admitted what she had done, proudly declaring that she had rid the world of a drunk driver that didn't deserve to live.

The tenants of the Seaside Center, their friends, and families were now gathered at the Tipsy Pirate, anxious to find out what would happen to the shopping plaza and their leases.

"The lawyer had this letter couriered to me, but he'll also email copies to each of you." Scooter shuffled through the pages. "It's full of lots of legal jargon, which I'll summarize. Basically, the new owner of the Seaside Center has decided not to terminate your leases. It will take time for all the paperwork to work its way through the legal system, but, long story short, you don't have to worry about your businesses."

Everyone cheered and toasted the good news. Then the florist tentatively raised her hand.

"Who's the new owner?" she asked.

Scooter rubbed his chin. "That's the interesting thing. It's Francine Murphy."

"Francine?" Alejandra asked, wide-eyed. "But how?"

"Why don't you explain, my little qutrit," Scooter said. "You know all the details better than anyone."

Everyone looked expectantly at me. I took a sip of my gin and tonic, then folded my hands in front of me. "It turns out that Robert Ronaldo was the father of Francine's illegitimate daughter. He never acknowledged her when she was born. That was back when he was known as George 'Jumping Sassafras' Jones."

"Jumping Sassafras?" Ben asked.

"That's the name he went by when he was a boxer in St. Louis. He used to come into Francine's nail salon for manicures. They ended up having an affair, and one thing led to another."

Josefina frowned. "Why didn't he marry her?"

"Mama, not everyone gets married when they get pregnant," Alejandra said gently.

"Humph," was Josefina's only response.

Eduardo patted his wife's arm, then asked, "My little girl's nail salon is safe?"

"Yes. Apparently, Francine felt so bad about what she did to your son …" Scooter paused to nod at Miguel, … that she ripped up the paperwork terminating everyone's leases."

The bookstore owner furrowed his brow. "But the day of our protest march, Cassie said that she didn't have the power to reverse the terminations and the new leases had already been signed. It was a done deal."

"That was a lie," I said. "Just one of many she told. She knew she could make more money leasing the shopping center to chain stores then to local businesses."

The florist raised her hand again. "I don't understand. Did Cassie leave the Seaside Center to Francine?"

I leaned forward. "That's exactly what happened. Remember how Francine and Angus both claimed to have seen Miguel that night?"

Everyone turned and looked at Angus. He slumped down in his chair sheepishly. I had been surprised when he showed up at the Tipsy Pirate. Most of the tenants had given him the cold shoulder, but the florist stunned us all when she patted the seat next to her and invited him to sit down.

When the owner of the bookstore told him to get lost, she stuck up for Angus, saying that he knew what he had done was wrong, but that he had done it for the right reasons. Everyone demanded an explanation, but when he refused to defend himself, the florist snapped.

"His mother is seriously ill. She can't afford treatment, and she'll die unless she gets it. So when Cassie offered him an astronomical sum of money to lie about who killed her husband, Angus agreed. He's her only child. What would you have done if it was your mother?"

No one said anything. Then the waitress deposited a platter of mixed appetizers and a dessert sampler platter on the table. Everyone busied themselves fighting over the egg rolls, fried cheese balls, chocolate cupcakes, and cheesecake bars.

"Hey, wait a minute," Ben said. "You

never did explain about how Francine ended up with the Seaside Center."

I wiped pineapple dipping sauce off my lips with my napkin, then continued my story. "Well, Cassie thought it would be more believable if someone who wasn't a tenant also claimed to have seen Miguel, you know, um ..." I cleared my throat. "Anyway, she knew that Robert had fathered Francine's child. So, Cassie promised that if Francine did what she wanted, then she'd change her will so that Francine and her daughter would inherit."

"That doesn't sound ideal," Penny said. "Francine would have to wait until Cassie died to inherit."

I shrugged. "It probably seemed like the best deal she could make. She didn't care much about herself, but she knew eventually, her daughter and grandchildren would be taken care of."

"Sounds like a motive for murder to me," Ben blurted out. He glanced at

Scooter, who was desperately looking for chocolate. "Sorry, buddy."

"That's what I originally thought when I heard about Cassie's updated will," I said. "But Francine was nowhere near Coconut Cove the day of the auditions. She had an air-tight alibi."

"Well, however it happened, I'm glad that Francine decided to do the right thing," the bookstore owner said.

"Hear, hear," the deli owner said.

"I'm not sure I can forgive her for what she did to my brother though," Alejandra muttered.

Miguel leaned over, whispered something in her ear, then kissed her cheek. Standing up, he held up his glass. "I'd like to propose a toast to everyone who stood behind me and my family. It means the world to us."

Eduardo and Josefina smiled, expressing their gratitude before enveloping their son in an embrace.

Alejandra got to her feet next. Raising

her wineglass, she said, "Here's to the tenants of the Seaside Center. We managed to keep Coconut Cove local!"

Everyone joined in the toast, cheering so loudly that pretty soon everyone in the bar joined in.

"I think we deserve our own private celebration," Scooter said to me quietly.

"For solving the murders of Robert Ronaldo and Cassie Newton?" I asked.

Scooter shuddered, then pulled his plate toward him. After scraping the last of the chocolate off and quickly eating it, he took a deep breath.

"Better?" He nodded. "Sorry. That was my fault. I shouldn't have said that word out loud."

"When I said we should celebrate, I meant the fact that we survived fixing our anchor light."

"Not to mention got rid of the mud dauber nest," I said.

"Exactly. We haven't been out for a really nice meal in a long time. Probably since our wedding anniversary. What do you say we get all dressed up and go to Chez Poisson tomorrow night?"

* * *

The next night, we were having a drink at the Chez Poisson bar while we waited for our table. "You look so handsome," I said, running my hands down his jacket lapels. "I can't remember the last time I saw you in a suit."

"That's one of the advantages of running your own business. I can dress more casually then when I worked for a big company. And living in Florida means that usually involves shorts and flip-flops."

"As long as it doesn't involve pompoms."

He pulled me into an embrace. "Admit it, my little qutrit, you loved that costume."

"I think you might want to come up

with a new pet name for me," I said.

"Why? Qutrit is adorable, just like you are."

"Yes, but everyone asks what it means, and it's way too complicated to explain."

"Just wear your pompom costume. It always helps to explain physics concepts with props."

"Unfortunately, Mrs. Moto has turned the pompoms into her new cat toys."

Scooter smirked. "Let me guess. You gave them to her."

"No comment."

A waiter approached us, telling us our table was ready. As we walked through the dining room, I gasped.

"Look over there," I whispered to Scooter. "Elvis is in the house."

"Elvis? What are you talking about ... oh, is that who I think it is?"

I squeezed Scooter's hand. "This is so exciting. He's going to propose to Anabel and we have front row seats."

Scooter put his hand on my lower back and steered us toward our table. As he pulled out my chair for me, he said, "I'm pretty sure Chief Dalton wasn't expecting an audience though."

"Then he shouldn't have chosen a public place."

Scooter chuckled. "By audience, I meant you."

I propped our menus in front of us, partially hiding us from view. "Fine. Let's give him some privacy."

Then we sipped on champagne and watched the show. The chief cleared his throat, then got to his feet. He pulled a velvet box out of the pocket of his sequined jumpsuit. Anabel put her hands to her mouth, her eyes wide. As the burly man knelt next to her, a hush fell over the diners.

"Anabel, you're the love of my life and I can't imagine spending another day without you. The biggest mistake I ever made was letting you go." He paused to open the jewelry box, his hands shaking. Holding up her old engagement ring—now sparkling from having been cleaned—he looked Anabel in the eyes. "Will you do me the honor of becoming my wife ... again?"

It was the longest speech I had ever heard him make.

Anabel said yes, tears streaming down her face, and the room broke out in applause.

I stood and did a fist pump in the air, cheering loudly. Both the chief and Anabel spun around looking in our direction. She grinned when she saw me. The chief, well, he didn't exactly smile at me, but he didn't scowl either, so I considered that to be a win.

While the couple embraced, I looped my arm through Scooter's. "Looks like we have a wedding to help plan. Do you think they would want to get married on a sailboat?"

AUTHOR'S NOTE AND ACKNOWLEDGMENTS

Thank you so much for reading my book! If you enjoyed it, I'd be grateful if you would consider leaving a short review on the site where you purchased it. Reviews help other readers find my books and encourage me to keep writing.

My experiences buying my first sailboat with my husband in New Zealand (followed by our second sailboat in the States), learning how to sail, and living aboard our boats inspired me to write the Mollie McGhie Sailing Mysteries. You might say that there's a little bit of Mollie in me.

One of the things I like about being a writer is weaving in my own experiences into my books, such as the scene where Mollie goes up the mast and is attacked by mud daubers. We needed to send someone up the mast of our sailboat, *Tickety Boo*, and guess who got elected? Yep, lucky old me. I have a fear of heights so it wasn't something I was looking forward to, but I knew that it had to be done, so I strapped myself into the bosun's chair and headed on up. When I got to the top, I made the mistake of looking down. Everyone looks so small when you're that high up in the air. Then the mud daubers attacked. I might have screamed a little. Intellectually, I knew they weren't likely to sting me, but still, we're talking about wasps here. Eek! I finally did make it down, unscathed, gobbled down some chocolate, and swore never to do that again. Spoiler alert: I did go up the mast again. Much easier the second time around.

I want to thank my husband, Scott Jacobson, for reading earlier drafts and providing insightful and thoughtful feedback, as well as his unfailing support and encouragement. So many of the humorous moments in this book are directly inspired by him. Many thanks as well to my editor, Alecia at Under Wraps Publishing, for being so easy to work with and for her great suggestions.

For updates on new releases, my current projects, sales and promotions, and other fun stuff, you can sign up for my newsletter at ellenjacobsonauthor.com/newsletter.

ABOUT THE AUTHOR

Ellen Jacobson is a chocolate obsessed cat lover who writes cozy mysteries and romantic comedies. After living on a sailboat for many years, she now travels around in a teeny-tiny camper with her husband and an imaginary cat named Simon.

Her Mollie McGhie cozy mystery series, featuring a reluctant sailor turned amateur sleuth, is inspired by her own sailing adventures and misadventures living aboard sailboats in New Zealand and the States.

Her Smitten with Travel romantic comedy series is inspired by her life as an expat in Scotland and New Zealand and passion for exploring new countries and learning about new cultures.

Find out more at ellenjacobsonauthor.com

ALSO BY ELLEN JACOBSON

The Mollie McGhie Sailing Mystery Series

Robbery at the Roller Derby (Prequel)
Murder at the Marina (Book #1)
Bodies in the Boatyard (Book #2)
Poisoned by the Pier (Book #3)
Dead in the Dinghy (Book #4)
Shooting by the Sea (Book #5)

The Smitten with Travel
Romantic Comedy Series

Smitten with Ravioli (Book #1)
Smitten with Croissants (Book #2)

Made in the USA
Monee, IL
15 May 2021